Choose your Lane to love!

Readers love
AMY LANE

Immortal

"…a fantastically rendered story of an extraordinary passion that echoes beyond the mortal world."

—Joyfully Jay

"…a gorgeous novel, eloquent in its joy and sorrow, hopeful in its promise of forever, meaningful in the way of fairy tales that teach us we are each the crucibles of love, and love is the conqueror of hate."

—The Novel Approach

Candy Man

"Oh God…. I friggin LOVE Amy Lane!!! This book broke my heart wide open, and then filled it with kittens, puppies, candy, and most importantly love! It was so perfect!!!!"

—Love Bytes

"…this book was nothing short of amazing… if you haven't read it yet, go do it RIGHT NOW."

—MM Good Book Reviews

Beneath the Stain

"Amy Lane at her best…"

—Prism Book Alliance

By AMY LANE

Behind the Curtain
Beneath the Stain
Bewitched by Bella's Brother
Bolt-hole
Christmas with Danny Fit
Clear Water
Do-over
Food for Thought
Gambling Men: The Novel
Going Up!
Grand Adventures (Dreamspinner Anthology)
Hammer & Air
If I Must
Immortal
It's Not Shakespeare
Left on St. Truth-be-Well
The Locker Room
Mourning Heaven
Phonebook
Puppy, Car, and Snow
Racing for the Sun
Raising the Stakes
Shiny!
Sidecar
A Solid Core of Alpha
Super Sock Man
Tales of the Curious Cookbook
Three Fates (Multiple Author Anthology)
Truth in the Dark
Turkey in the Snow
Under the Rushes
Winter Ball
Wishing on a Blue Star (Dreamspinner Anthology)

Published by DREAMSPINNER PRESS
www.dreamspinnerpress.com

By Amy Lane (cont)

Published by Dreamspinner Press
www.dreamspinnerpress.com

Winter Ball
Amy Lane

Published by

DREAMSPINNER PRESS

5032 Capital Circle SW, Suite 2, PMB# 279, Tallahassee, FL 32305-7886 USA
www.dreamspinnerpress.com

ISBN: 978-1-62380-797-9
Digital ISBN: 978-1-62380-898-3
Library of Congress Control Number: 2015947603
First Edition December 2015

Printed in the United States of America
∞
This paper meets the requirements of
ANSI/NISO Z39.48-1992 (Permanence of Paper).

To Mate, especially this time, because Mate is like Skipper. He didn't imagine himself a leader, but he became one because he loved the game. And to my three kids in soccer, because it's part of their blood, and my one who took karate instead, because he still knows that feeling of belonging that a sport can give you.

And to Mary, who, when I pointed out that this story was Cinderella from the prince's point of view and that Winter Ball was almost a pun, almost cried. Because yes. Everybody should have his or her own fairy tale, just for them, and a Happy Ever After.

Illuminate the Goal

SCOGGINS WAS at it again.

"Offsides? I wasn't offsides! You assholes wouldn't know offsides if it walked up and bit you on the—"

"Ass?" Skipper Keith supplied dryly. "C'mon, Richie, you're gonna get a red card. Can we just play some fuckin' soccer?"

Scoggins rolled his eyes and muttered under his breath, but he settled down. Skip had always held that sort of power over Richie, and everybody on the team knew it. "Yeah, fine, but that redheaded linebacker shoulders me in the ribs one more time, all bets are off."

The redhead was nearly six eight. Slow as a drugged and lumbering milk cow, yes, but effective. Nobody wanted to go up against him for the ball, and Skipper had his own bruises that no shin guard could protect against.

"I'll take him," Skipper said, because he was bigger than Richie, for one, and because he knew it wasn't personal for another. Richie Scoggins's hair was as red as the other team's defender's, and his temper—holy shit, was it hot.

They lined up for the ball, and Scoggins took center and made the pass. Skipper suddenly had a clear run up the field, the westering sun in the chill October evening casting an ethereal path to the god of the goal.

Skipper and Scoggins, they were true believers.

Dribble, dribble, pass, dodge, dribble—they'd been playing together since tech school, when Skipper walked into a computer class they'd shared with a flyer for rec league adult soccer. They'd both had jobs. Neither one of them had time to play for the school team, but rec league? *That* they could do.

1

Six years later, they worked their separate jobs and did this: practiced and played soccer every Thursday evening, essentially with the same guys they'd played with since tech school.

Knowing the team comforted Skipper. *Winning* with them exhilarated him.

"Scoggins!" he called, seeing his way blocked, and Scoggins was right *there*, ready to take the ball. Skip pulled back to avoid the offside charge and let Scoggins go for it, hauling ass, dodging the big Scottish warrior to his left, wily little Menendez (the traitor who used to play for their team) on his right, and he kicked! Very nice—he lofted the ball up, up, and up....

"*Goal!*" Scoggins screamed, arms above his head. "Goal! Goal! Goal! The Scorpions have won again!" Not technically true— they still had some time left, but just as Skipper opened his mouth to say that...

...the ref blew the whistle to end the game.

Much cheering ensued: hugging, hand-clasping, backslapping, butt-slapping, and sweaty male bodies hopping around to keep warm in the chill. Finally they grabbed their sweatshirts from the sidelines and walked off the slightly swampy middle school field with the irregular grass, and up the rise to their cars.

Where they proceeded to break a couple of rules by digging into the ice chest in the back of Richie Scoggins's Honda Accord.

The party was equal opportunity—the fall rec league season had ended with this game. There was nothing left but the tournament over the weekend (where the Scorpions would probably get slaughtered, because they were up against a lot of guys who'd played in college instead of tech school and who practiced three times a week instead of just one) and the inevitable question.

"Yo!" Menendez threw out, wiping his face with the back of his hand. In the daytime, he worked up in Folsom at Intel, but down here in Citrus Heights, he used words like *yo*. "Are we doing winter ball this year?"

"I don't know," Skipper threw back. "You gonna play with us?"

Menendez grimaced. He'd signed up late this quarter and had gotten put on the Dirty Dogs. That big Scottish warrior had hogged the ball a lot. "I am if we sign up this week!" he said, hauling his fingers through his curls. "Man, tell me we can play ball again. I know all you guys got family, but soccer's, like, the only thing to get me through the holidays!"

Scoggins tapped Skipper's back gently, and Skipper nodded. Yeah, Scoggins had family, but Skipper had met them more than once when he'd gone to pick him up for the movies or to go out on a Friday night. Some family was worse than no family.

Which was what Skipper had. His parents had split when he was twelve, his dad was incommunicado, and his mom had died of liver cirrhosis right after he got out of school.

"I feel ya," he said, then looked around to the other twelve guys he played with. Skipper's real name was Christopher. The team called him Skipper because that first quarter, their coach had bailed, and Skip had sort of captained that ship.

"What do you say, guys? We only need ten and a goalie, so if some of you got kids and in-laws and shit this Christmas, you can bail."

Three of them *did* bail, but that left Cooper, McAlister, Thomas, Galvan, Owens, Jefferson, Jimenez, Singh, Menendez, and Scoggins—so, one for sub.

There was a round of high fives and a toast with everyone's mostly empty beer, and Skipper made a mental note to start the paperwork the next day.

"I'll remind you," Scoggins said as the last of the guys wandered away, leaving them alone. Full night had fallen, and Richie shivered. He was the only one who hadn't brought a sweatshirt.

Skipper had parked right next to him—their two silver Honda Accords bore the butt prints of pretty much every guy on the team at this point—and he reached into the back of his car and hauled out his black zip-up hoodie, then threw it at Richie because he hated to see Richie cold.

3

Richie didn't get a lot of mothering—or fathering for that matter—even though he pretty much ran his parents' junkyard business. He showed up, did the accounts, got bitched at for not helping on the jobs, and kept the business afloat. Someone needed to take care of Richie. Skipper had seen that even when they were in school. Richie was a good guy—would stay up late to help friends study, always brought the beer or the chips or the water bottles, and didn't mind being coskipper to a group of guys who just wanted to fucking play.

"That's fine," Skipper muttered, yawning. "You remind me. Tomorrow's gonna be our team building anyway—"

"Where you going?" Richie asked, entranced as always by Skipper's few corporate perks.

Skipper had tried to tell him that the tech firm he worked for wasn't particularly glamorous, but for Richie? Anything that didn't involve working with your parents was absolutely top-of-the-line. In a way, it gave Skip a good perspective—everybody got frustrated at work. It was important to remember that he was doing something he was good at, got promotions and raises regularly, and his boss didn't have the legal right to call him a dumbshit just because she married his father.

"Bowling," Skip said, finishing off his beer and rounding up the empties. There was a can collection bin by the school. So far nobody had complained about the neatly bagged beer cans once a week, and Skip was going to keep his fingers crossed. He *liked* this league, but the one beer after the practices or games gave him a social group he just didn't get at work, so it was a risk he was willing to take.

"Bowling?" Richie sounded tickled. "Seriously? Can I come?"

Skip looked at him: five foot eight of wiry, fierce competitor, and suddenly he sounded like a little girl. "Can you come what? Bowling?"

Richie nodded. "Yeah. I got nothing better to do with my Friday night, and my dad and Kay used to go. I was pretty fucking good, you know?"

4

It was the first time Richie had ever said anything even remotely pleasant about his parents. "You break up with whatserface?"

"Melanie? Yeah. She's history."

Richie was still bouncing on his toes and blowing on his fingers. Skip motioned for him to get in his car. "I'll sit, we can shoot the shit, 'kay?"

Why not? Skip had the keys to the gate and the coaching paperwork in his car. They could stay there a while before anybody got upset about the two cars parked in front of the middle school.

Richie nodded gratefully and they hurried up and slid in. Skip had to shove the car seat back to accommodate his legs—they'd both bought their cars right out of tech school because of a graduating student discount, but sometimes Skip dreamed of the next-sized car up. Six foot one didn't feel that tall until you were sitting in the front of a compact car.

Richie's car was comfortably rumpled. There were a couple of fast-food bags under Skip's feet, but not too many, and a gym bag and a towel in the back. Skipper had given him a reusable aluminum mug for his coffee in the morning, and that sat in the cup holder, needing to be washed.

Richie turned the key just enough to power the stereo, and then fiddled with his phone until an alternative mix came up. Milky Chance's "Down by the River" played, and Skip relaxed into it, loving the song and the feeling of autumn that came with it.

"So," he said after the dance of opening chords washed over him, "Melanie."

Richie let out a sigh. "She's not... I mean, she was nice, and we had fun and all, but...." He shrugged. "Not... you know...."

Yeah. Skip knew. Most of Richie's relationships went like this. He met a girl, they went out on a few dates, saw some movies, ate some dinners, even went to the occasional concert, and then, just when it got to be serious, after the first couple of sleepovers, the relationship ended.

"Man," Skip said, "it's not fair to these girls, you know? I mean, you want no strings, find a girl who wants no strings too. There's no shame in that."

5

Richie blew out a breath. "Yeah. Well, it's not even that I don't want strings. In fact, I *want* strings. I'd *love* strings. I got these dreams, you know?"

Skipper looked at him avidly, his bony cheeks and full lips fully visible in silhouette, illuminated by the sodium lamp outside. "No," he said, fascinated. "Seriously. Tell me about the dreams."

Because they were guys, right? They talked about soccer and their shitty jobs and Richie's terrible parents. They went to concerts and out to movies and out for beers after the games, and hung out at each other's places playing Xbox and planning the ultimate LAN party that they were both fairly sure would never happen because they were too busy with soccer.

But they didn't talk about their dreams. Did men talk about their dreams together?

Did Skipper have any dreams besides playing next to Richie?

Richie blew out a breath and grabbed a bottle of water from the flat behind Skip's seat. The movement brought them in contact, and in the darkened car, Skip was suddenly very… aware.

Very aware of Richie's small, freckled body.

Skip had seen that small freckled body ripped with muscle, sheening with sweat, charging across the soccer field in the sun. Richie's shoulders were burned from doing that too much, but you could count every rib and every muscle group, because there wasn't an ounce to spare on Richie.

That body was right next to Skip's in the car's small confines, and Skip had a hard time pushing back an uncomfortable… thing. Ruthlessly he stomped on it until it was of manageable size to hide, but that didn't mean it wasn't still there.

Richie turned and handed Skip the water; then he grabbed another one for himself.

This time Skip was just inches from his neck.

Richie smelled like sweat, and Skip found himself wondering: if he licked that pale strip of skin in the moonlight, would it be salty? Would Richie crack him across the face with an elbow, or would he shudder, sigh, and melt? Skipper thought that if Richie ever put his lips on *Skip's* neck, Skip would probably shudder, sigh, and melt.

Right now, as Richie leaned back in his seat, Skipper was trying really hard not to shudder.

"So," Skip said, keeping his voice even with an effort. "Melanie? Dreams?"

Richie cracked open his bottle of water and drank deep. When he was done, he wiped his mouth with the back of his hand and let out a breath. "I want strings," he murmured to himself. "I do. I just… you know. I sleep with the girl, and the next day, she's all vulnerable, and I'm all nice to her, and I think, 'I can do this. I can take care of this girl. She's a nice girl, and we had fun,' you know?"

Skip thought back to his last relationship. It had been a while. Oh yeah. Amber of the brown hair and the tight T-shirts and ass-enhancing jeans.

God, she'd been fun. A wicked sense of humor, a filthy mouth, and an obsession with rimming Skip until he came.

Not even thinking about the rim job could make Skip hard, and that was sort of unnatural. That had been part of the reason he'd broken up with her. Yeah, he'd given the requisite reciprocation in bed, but it had felt very… very much like he was filling out an invoice and rendering payment for services performed.

Amber had really loved sex, and Skip hadn't. It felt like a cheat, really, being with a girl when she was going all out and Skip was going through the motions. Amber had cried the last time they'd been in bed together. *I get in bed feeling all sexual and attractive, and I don't know what you do, Skip, but you make me feel slutty and ashamed.*

That was no good.

So Skip got it. He got what Richie was saying. "Yeah," he responded into the quiet. "I get it. You think, 'Nice girl. I like her a lot.'"

"Yeah!" Richie looked at him, big green eyes shiny and colorless in the light. "You *do*. But something about touching them—you know. Guys at school going off on boobs—I remember that. I remember being *so excited* when I got to see my first boob. I'd been jerking off,

7

like, three times a day, just because that thing sprang up and I needed to keep it down, right?"

Skipper stared. "Jesus, Richie, were you going for a record or something?"

"What? Three times a day?"

"Yeah. It takes me too long to get hard—I couldn't do it. But you were saying about girls...."

"Well, I thought I'd be so excited, seeing boobs, and Sierra Donovan showed me hers. I totally expected, like, super boner, you know? But there she was, shirt pulled up, boobs... boobing... and I got... nothin'." He shivered at the memory. "I went through the motions, used my mouth, was real gentle, she even let me put my hand down her pants, which was good, 'cause she came and she walked away happy."

"But you?" Skipper asked. He shifted in his seat, because embarrassingly enough, imagining Richie, a teenager, stroking someone else's naked flesh was actually making him a little hard. Usually that didn't happen unless he was alone in the dark, touching himself.

"I... I didn't get a stiffie until I got home that night," Richie said thoughtfully, gazing at his hands on the steering wheel. "And... and it's like that with all the girls. It's gotta be in the dark and it's gotta be closing my eyes and just feeling their hands on me. But in the morning, I look at them and...."

"Yeah," Skipper muttered. "I get that too."

Silence fell. The heater wasn't on, and Richie shuddered, probably because the car was cold inside. Skip went to pull his sweatshirt over his head, because he always ran a little hot.

"No!" Richie protested. "Skip, man, you don't gotta give me the shirt off your back."

Skipper paused because taking the sweatshirt off was awkward in the car. "That's good," he mumbled through the folds of fleece. "'Cause I'm stuck."

Richie laughed and slid his hands up Skip's arms, trying to untangle him from the damn sweatshirt, and Skip struggled and

8

fumbled, trying not to clock Richie in the face or anything. It was a short tussle, but that didn't stop Richie's hands from skimming his ribs, his stomach, his chest, his neck. Little touches, impersonal probably, but by the time Skip had wrestled off the damned sweater, he was sweaty, breathless, and, irony of ironies, hard.

He wadded up his sweatshirt and shoved it in his lap.

"Hey!" Richie laughed, grabbing for it. "After all that effort, I'll take the frickin' shi—" His hand brushed Skipper's crotch, and they locked gazes. "…irt?"

Skip closed his eyes, leaned back his head, and moaned. "Please don't think I'm weird," he mumbled. "Please. Just… you were talking about sex and then—hey!"

Richie stroked his dick through his shorts again, and everything in Skip's body tingled.

"Sorry," Richie mumbled, but he didn't sound sorry at all. "That's just…." He took one finger and started at Skip's groin, then ran a touch up the length of the thing as it was mashed to Skip's body under the soccer shorts and Under Armour. Richie got to the tip and his finger caught on the ridge through three layers of clothing, and Skip moaned again, closing his eyes.

"If you're so sorry," he whispered, "stop touching it! I'm embarrassed enou—"

Richie caught Skip's hand and brought it to his crotch.

Before Skip even knew what he was touching, his hand closed around a hard cock pushing against Richie's underwear just like Skip's was.

Skip's eyes flew open, and he and Richie regarded each other tensely in the dim light. For a heartbeat Skip thought the moment was over—Richie pulled back just a notch, and his hand relaxed on Skip's prick.

And something in Skip must have really wanted the moment to go on, because *his* hand tightened. Richie closed his eyes and parted his full lips….

Skip wanted to taste him more than he'd ever wanted to taste anything in his life.

That first brush of lips was so soft it almost didn't happen, but it *did*, and Richie didn't jerk away or protest or complain, so the second one went a little harder.

Richie's lips were a little rough, but Skip teased the seam of them with his tongue, and when he opened his mouth, the inside felt softer, like a girl's, but with this incredible *heat*.

Skip was cold—he'd given up his sweatshirt, and he wanted that heat.

He pushed forward, swept his tongue in, felt Richie's response. A shudder racked him, taking no prisoners, and he clenched his hand around Richie's cock, almost like he was holding on for dear life.

Richie moaned and fumbled at Skip's soccer shorts. Skip sucked in a breath, and Richie's clever little hand slid inside and then beneath the Under Armour, which he flipped down with a tight elastic *thwack*. Skip's cock sat exposed and quivering in the sensitizing chill.

And then Richie slid his hot, rough hand over the cap and squeezed the shaft.

Skip whimpered into his mouth, helpless.

Richie pulled his head back. "Grab mine," he commanded.

Skip angled his body so he could use both hands to strip Richie's shorts and Under Armour down under his ass. He held Richie firm with one hand on his hip and then snuck a peek to make sure he was giving Richie's fireplug dick a firm and hearty handshake.

Richie moaned and his cock pulsed in Skip's hand.

Skip closed his eyes again—he had to, because the shudder that rocked him at the feeling of warm flesh in his palm, *that* was too big to endure with eyes wide open.

A breath of air caught Skip's leaking cockhead, and the frisson of yearning that shook his body alarmed him on some level. *I need. I need I need I need....*

He didn't think he was the kind of guy to need. Amber had called him cold—he was pretty sure most of his girlfriends could agree with that. But Richie's mouth was hot and open, and his cock seared the skin of Skip's palm.

Richie's hand started to jerk almost spasmodically, but Skip felt the rhythm he was trying for. He whispered, "Sh... sh" against Richie's cheek and took that small, bony, rough hand in his own and taught him to stroke, a little slower, a little smoother.... *Oh! Oh yeah!*

"Skipper," Richie begged, and Skip moved his hand back to where it belonged.

Hard and a little slower, smoother. Richie's every moan, every whimper, drove Skipper up another notch into the unexpected inferno of passion that had opened up in Richie's Honda Accord.

The music changed from Milky Chance to Mumford & Sons, and as the guitars and banjo and keyboard raced to a pinnacle, a sharp, pounding drive in Skipper's stomach told him he was going to do the same.

Richie gasped, and a spurt of hot precome scalded Skipper's fingers. Skipper wanted... wanted... oh Jesus... he wanted so much from this moment, from Richie, from....

He moved his hand off Richie's hip to his jaw and positioned him for a kiss, a wild, passionate plundering. Richie kept stroking his cock, every callus a delicious bout of friction, every hard-handed squeeze *exactly* what Skipper needed.

Uh... uh... oh God, Richie's calluses caught on Skip's ridge, and it felt so... so good... so....

His entire body tingled, even his elbows and his scalp, and then his taint and his ass and his nipples and... tingling, tightening, cranked until breaking, and... oh... oh... oh....

Richie came for real, his body arching and bucking until he broke the kiss and his come, sticky and creamy and practically boiling with the heat from that furious little body, ran down the backs of Skipper's fingers, made his grip messy and smooth, and *that* did it. He arched his ass off the car seat, closed his eyes, and let the tingling take over his entire body, let it ride him, saw stars, and came.

He kept his eyes closed while his breathing adjusted. When he opened them, Richie was right there, his face inches away, his mouth swollen with Skipper's kisses, cheeks reddened from Skipper's stubble, eyes wide and shiny and shaken.

Skipper probably looked the same.

They stared at each other for a weighted moment. Skipper let go of Richie's cock at the same time Richie let go of his.

"Here," Richie muttered, reaching into one of the fast-food bags. He pulled out a handful of napkins and gave some to Skip. Skip looked at them dumbly. Richie, using gentle movements, took his own napkins and wiped off Skipper's cock.

"Oh," Skipper said, feeling dense.

"Here, Skip, lift up your hips."

Skip did, and Richie pulled his shorts up.

"Thanks. Do you want me to—" He gestured vaguely with the napkins, and then realized Richie's come was still running from his hand.

He stopped, mesmerized, and then, almost like he couldn't help it, he moved his hand to his mouth and sucked on the webbing between his thumb and forefinger.

It was salty and bitter, just like Skip's own come (boys tasted, just because), but something about how raw it was, tasting Richie like this, rocked Skip, cracked him open to the core, and he shuddered, almost pulling his knees up to his chest, because his groin ached fiercely, and he almost thought he could come again from the taste of Richie's fluids on his hand.

He opened his eyes and Richie was close in the confines of the car. He took Skip's hand and searched for the places Skip hadn't gotten, then started licking, very slowly, very deliberately, until Skip's fingers were clean.

Skip whimpered again. Oh hell. He wanted. He most definitely wanted again. But shouldn't they say something? Do something? Oh God, he and Richie had just kissed and given each other hand jobs and…. Skip's whole body screamed at him.

We must do this again. We must *do this again.*

"Richie," he gasped, breathy because Richie's tongue was still wiggling on the back of his knuckles. "Wh—" *What do you want to do? What did we just do? Why haven't we done this before? What are we going to do now? What does this all mean?*

"Bowling," Richie said, like he couldn't catch his breath either.

"Bowling?" Skip's chest hurt with the unspoken questions.

"I'll see you tomorrow," Richie said, nodding like Skip was slow and not catching on.

"Wh—"

Richie's thumb was covered in ejaculate, and he shoved it into Skip's mouth. Skip closed his lips around it, flattened his tongue, and sucked hard. His own come filled his senses, and oh, how bad did he want Richie's again?

"Tomorrow," Richie repeated, like he was insisting. "We'll get dinner. I'll come to your place and watch movies afterward. Tomorrow."

He was nodding, so Skip nodded too.

He pulled away from Richie's thumb, scraping the underside lightly with his teeth.

"Tomorrow," he said breathily. He couldn't seem to get a good lungful. His whole body refused to cooperate.

He needed to get out of there.

He leaned forward and pecked Richie chastely on the lips, then grabbed his sweater, which had fallen to the floor, and bolted out of the car. He paused with the door open, feeling bereft, feeling relieved.

"Tomorrow?" he asked, suddenly needing to hear it again.

"I promise," Richie said, searching Skipper's eyes intently.

"Good." Skipper nodded.

Richie seemed to see what he'd been looking for, because he smiled, and Skipper shut the door, tugged on his sweatshirt, and hopped into his own car as Richie turned the ignition.

First Kickoff

"You GOT a girl comin' tonight?" Clay Carpenter looked at him funny, and Skipper uneasily pulled out the collar of his green polo shirt.

"No," he said shortly, tossing his squishy brain-shaped stress ball in the air and keeping an eye open for his phone line. He and the other IT guys all had a rhythm down—you exercised, threw shit in the air, fiddled, fidgeted, and fucked off, right until your phone line rang, and then you did all of that *and* answered boring questions about how Grok make computer go.

"You shaved. You're blond—I don't see stubble until a week after you shave, and you have a jaw out of a DC comic book. There's no reason for you to shave. What's the fuckin' deal?"

Skipper turned to eyeball Carpenter, who was, as usual, out of standard dress code in a baseball jersey and sweats. Carpenter was a big guy—order the extra-special chair big—but he was also dry, funny, and he had a fondness for adorable kitten videos. Skip had once watched him spend a quarter of his paycheck on Doctors Without Borders when an earthquake hit Nepal, because he'd seen something in the disaster footage that had broken his heart. (Skip had never asked what, but he'd pitched in $100 himself, just to make Carpenter feel better.) Skip brought him soy lattes and bran muffins in an effort to help him slim down, but when Carpenter let out a bellow and a screech against his never-ending diet, Skip would go out and fetch his cheeseburger too. He was a friend, not a judge, and whatever Carpenter's deep-seated emotional issues with food, he was a genuinely good man.

But Skipper wasn't ready to talk about the night before, even to Carpenter.

14

"No girl," he muttered. "Just Richie." On the field, he was Scoggins. In person, *as* a person, he was Richie.

To Carpenter, who was a friend, he was Richie.

Odd how Skip had never thought of that before.

Carpenter smiled and paused, then pushed the Talk button on his phone. "Yes, ma'am. Did you turn it off? And then on. Yes, ma'am, reboot it. No, ma'am, I don't know why it works, maybe it needs a nap. Thank you so much for calling tech support!" Then he looked up at his screen. "Ooh! I gotta chatterer here. Why aren't *you* getting any calls?"

Skipper shrugged. Inside he was thinking that he usually walked his clients through consolidating their data, reinitializing their routers, and making sure they had compatible browsers. By the time Skipper was done with a caller, nothing on their computer would go wrong again, *ever*, so he didn't get a lot of repeat calls like Carpenter.

"I got no idea. Go, chatter."

"Yeah, sure, but I'm glad your soccer buddy is coming—you guys talk geek. I need more geek talkers at the bowling thing. God, sports, why?"

Skipper didn't have an answer—he wasn't on the social committee—but he actually thought bowling wasn't a bad idea. Of course, he didn't have a bad back and swollen feet either—Carpenter probably wasn't particularly comfortable bowling.

"I dunno, but feel free to talk *Halo* and *Titanfall* to your heart's content." Oop! There went his phone. "Tesko Tech Business Services, this is Skipper Keith, can I help you?"

He paused for a moment while a courteous, *educated* voice washed over him. Then he tried not to let his eyes bug out.

"No, sir, I'm not having one over on you. I didn't even *know* there was a dog called a skipper-kee. How do you spell that?"

Seriously? He did something totally alien then and picked up a pen, making careful note of the letters as the person on the other end of the line spelled them out.

S-c-h-i-p-p-e-r-k-e.

"Skipper Kee. Huh. Who knew. Well, in my case, my soccer team calls me Skipper, but my first name is Christopher and my last name is, well, Keith. So not 'key.' So, you know. Not a schipperke."

He had to ask the caller to repeat himself twice for the next part of the conversation.

And when he replied, Carpenter couldn't stop laughing.

"No!" Carpenter howled as the bowling balls crashed into pins all around them. "Richie, I shit you not! You should have heard him."

Skipper groaned, and Carpenter held his fist to his ear, thumb and little finger extended, before he did a passable imitation of Skipper.

"No, sir. I can assure you that no part of this Skipper Keith is black and fuzzy and aggressive either. Yes, that probably is a shame. Did you have any computer needs you wanted me to take care of?"

Richie looked up at Skipper and howled with laughter, clapping and stomping like Carpenter was a regular comedian.

Well, it *did* make a pretty good story, and frankly, Skipper had been so worried about seeing Richie again that he was grateful that Carpenter had been so eager to share. He'd paced in the lobby of the bowling alley, not caring that he looked like a nervous boyfriend, and as soon as Richie broke through from the chilly outside to the overheated inside, Skipper relaxed for the first time that day.

As Richie had drawn near and filled out the paperwork, Skipper got a whiff of cigarette smoke, and he bumped Richie's shoulder with his elbow and scowled. Richie had shrugged, staring at his receipt like it held the secrets of the universe.

"You know," he mumbled. "Rob and Paul smoke, my folks smoke, I take my break with them—I was nerv—"

And then Carpenter interrupted, which had been a blessing. Skipper hadn't wanted to have the "nervous" discussion with Richie when for the first time that day, Skipper *wasn't* nervous, and a curse because, well…

The story ended quite uncomfortably.

"So *that's* the best part?" Richie hooted, taking a swig of his beer.

"Nope!" Carpenter crowed. "The best part was this: 'I'm sorry sir, but you're not allowed to access porn from your work computer. No, sir. No, any porn, sir, not just gay porn.'" Carpenter grinned at Skipper, his broad, bearded face maniacal with glee. "No, sir, I think it would be a very bad idea if I came to your office and helped take down your firewall just for kicks."

"No!" Richie sputtered, and Skipper shook his head at Carpenter, threatening dire consequences.

"No, seriously?" Richie was so excited he set his beer down and stood up, hopping on his toes while they waited for the fourth person in their game to finish botching his spare. "He totally hit on you? I mean, you guys all work in one building—that's *insane*! What? Did he think you'd get there and start stripping like a Chippendales dancer?"

Skipper's whole body twitched in horror. "In front of a *stranger*?" he squeaked, and then he saw Richie's eyes on him, wide and mesmerized.

"I'm up!" Carpenter groaned, pushing himself to his feet with a sigh. He got his ball from the carousel as Wayans slunk back, dejected by the three-pin spare he'd missed.

Richie just kept looking at Skipper, lips slightly parted, hunger so transparent on his face that it was all Skipper could do not to just kiss him, taste him, tobacco and all, to answer that need.

"You're thinking about it," Skipper murmured under the sound of the balls and pins and the echoes of the alley.

"All night, I thought about it," Richie replied. Carpenter's whoop yanked them out of their own little world, and they stood up with Wayans to applaud Carpenter's strike—something he'd never done before.

Their team placed somewhere in the middle, but everybody knew the best part was pizza and beer afterward, so nobody complained about the score. Tesko Tech was a big enough company that the IT department didn't have to share team-building time with any of the actual execs, so everybody at the pizza parlor knew each other—and

Richie, because plus-ones were welcome and Skip asked him to these things a lot.

So it wasn't a date.

It was guys out with friends, cracking jokes and sharing work stories. Carpenter had a good one about the four-year-old who called because her mother had gone into the garage to do laundry and she thought that mommy had gone into the computer screen.

"How'd she know the number?" Richie asked, entranced.

"Apparently Mom had it taped to the computer screen—she's sort of a frequent flyer."

"Oh Lord," Wayans muttered. He passed a hand the color of teak wood over his shaved head. "I've got this one woman—I swear, she sounds just like my mother. I almost asked her if she grew up in New Orleans too. But it's like she's read a manual—a *manual* I tell you—of all the dumb things to do with a computer. She actually called me up once and asked me how to disconnect a wireless mouse. It was insane."

General laughter then—and of course one more person had a story.

But still, that didn't stop Skipper from yearning for that first person to leave. Just one person, that was all it took. C'mon, someone have a kid, or a wife, or a—

"I gotta go," Carpenter said, standing up resolutely and holding his hands out to ward off the evil pizza. "I've got a *WOW* event in fifteen minutes—Skip, you want to log on with me?"

Skip looked up, flattered, but shook his head. "Naw, Clay. I promised Richie a few games of *Titanfall* when we get back. Ready, Rich?"

Richie stood up, his movements so casual Skipper had to think that he, too, was quivering like a taut piano string.

Well, good. Every inch of Skipper's skin—every *millimeter*— was tingling and tight. His groin ached like a bruise or an abscessed tooth, and it was all he could do not to adjust himself as he swung his leg over the bench, grabbed his jacket, and headed for the door.

Walking out of the Round Table and into the chilly October night felt like a fifty-yard walk of shame in his underwear, and Skipper *still* had a woody when he got to his car. He stuck his face up to the sky for a moment when they got there, and he thought he smelled wood smoke in the air.

"What?" Richie asked, parked, as usual, right next to him.

"Can you smell that? It's gonna be Halloween on Sunday," he said happily.

"Yeah?"

"Yeah!" For the first time since he'd walked into the bowling alley, Skipper could look at him and not think about kissing or rough, bony hands wrapped around his cock.

"Maybe we go buy some candy and decorations tomorrow, yeah?" Richie asked, sounding enthusiastic.

Skipper beamed at him. After his parents had split, his mom had sort of let holidays slide off the map. Skipper remembered a lot of Christmases where his present was money to run and buy takeout, and a lot of Halloweens where he had to turn off the lights and hide under the bed so nobody knew he was home without any candy. Since he'd gotten out of tech school, he'd been assembling, little by little, his own boxes of holiday trappings. Maybe tomorrow he could get something for the front porch of his little house.

And Richie would come with him.

"Absolutely." Suddenly the evening ahead didn't have quite the tang of dread in it—there was going to be a tomorrow in which they lost a soccer tournament game first, and then visited the Spirit store for decorations and the Sam's Club for the two giant ten-pound bags of the really good candy. Whatever tonight brought, there was going to be a tomorrow with Richie. "Here, let's get to my house—you can crash there tonight and we can go shopping after the game."

A slow, gorgeous smile bloomed across Richie's bony, plain face. "Good idea, Skip. I brought a few changes of clothes just in case...."

They both stopped and looked at each other. Just in case what? Just in case he crashed over? Just in case they spent the night together?

Just in case they repeated what they'd done the night before?

19

They stared at each other over Richie's car, the silence between them breathless.

"See you at the house," Skip croaked at last, and Richie nodded.

As Skip slid behind the wheel, he found himself wondering if Richie was going to take this opportunity to bail.

HE NEEDN'T have worried.

Richie actually beat him to the house and was waiting on the porch with a gym bag over his shoulder. He looked around the neat little yard as Skip walked up.

"Nice fence—is that new?"

Skip smiled, pleased. "Yeah—got a kit from Lowe's."

Skip's neighborhood had been mostly For Sale signs three years ago when he'd first bought his house. He'd felt bad—the street was lower-middle-class, and a lot of folks had needed to foreclose, but he couldn't have waited. He and his mom had lived in an apartment, right up until she'd died, and he'd hated it. Hated not being able to paint the walls or determine what the outside would look like, or not even being able to buy his own overhead lights. When he'd been in high school, when he hadn't been working, he'd been dreaming about what his "grown-up" home would look like.

His mom had died when he'd been in tech school, leaving a tiny bit of savings he hadn't known about (and she probably hadn't either, or it would have been used on scotch by then), and he'd been able to get a first-time buyer's loan at a time when interest rates were at rock bottom.

He'd had his job for maybe three months before he'd started looking for a house he could afford.

What he'd ended up with was a tiny one-bedroom home in Carmichael, with a shitty heat and air system and a really vast backyard with a wooden patio actually built around an oak tree. It had taken him three years to get the backyard to a place where he was pretty sure it could keep a dog.

20

"Yeah," he said, not able to keep the smile from his face. "I sort of thought… you know, getting myself a dog for Christmas this year."

Richie stopped bouncing on his toes and frowned. "You give yourself Christmas presents?" he asked, like the thought had just occurred to him. Richie's parents usually gave him gift certificates for Christmas—often to places like Lowe's, because they wanted his help working on their house, since he rented the apartment over the garage.

"Who else is going to?" Skipper asked, genuinely puzzled. Men didn't give presents. His office had a gift exchange every year—and he'd been scrupulous about participating too. Last year Carpenter had been his designated giver, and his gift had been a really big gift certificate to Carpenter's favorite donut shop. Skipper had consoled himself with the knowledge that Carpenter *really* loved that donut shop, and the gift had been a true act of friendship.

Richie looked stricken. "Well, you know. This year… this year, I'll get you something."

That was sweet. "I'll get you something too," Skipper said, delighted, and turned to fumble with the key. "Careful—don't want to let Hazel out."

He pushed the door open and automatically stopped the entrance with his foot. Hazel, the fuzzy black cat that had sort of moved in when he started feeding her, snarled low in her throat and retreated. At first he'd wanted to let her be inside/outside, but the day after he let her out, he found her under the porch, meowing piteously, so very confused. He'd discovered that if he could keep her from escaping in the first place, she was usually content to lie low inside the house and sit on his lap during television time.

The front door opened straight into the living room, and he turned and plugged his phone into the charger that he kept there and put his keys in the bowl, making sure he left enough room for Richie to come in so he could set his stuff by the couch like he usually did.

The door shut behind him and he paused, hand over the bowl as he set his keys down. He heard the thump of Richie's duffel bag in the corner, by the bookshelf, and was going to turn to see why when

21

Richie plastered himself to Skipper's back, his body throwing off heat like an overheating computer tower.

Skip froze.

He heard a rustle, and Richie moved restlessly before hanging his Scorpions team windbreaker up on the hook. Then Richie's hands moved insistently at Skipper's cuffs.

"Rich—"

"Skip?" Richie sounded winded, like he was having trouble talking.

"Yeah?" Skipper couldn't do anything but whisper.

"You thought about last night any?"

Richie got the windbreaker off and then reached around Skipper, rucking up his shirt and sliding his palms up and down around Skipper's taut abdomen.

"Mmmm...." It wasn't an answer, but it most obviously wasn't a no.

"I've been thinking about it," Richie whispered. Skip hadn't flipped on the light, and Richie's growly voice, his breath between Skip's shoulder blades, his tight little body so hot and hard against Skip's back—how was he supposed to say no?

He groaned instead.

"Yeah. That's what I thought." Richie's hands on Skip's hips turned aggressive, whirling him around and shoving him against the doorframe. Richie stared at him in the dark, those eyes—damn. Big limpid pools of fucking want.

"Richie, I...."

"You what?" Richie demanded, but he punctuated the words by grinding his crotch up against Skip's thigh, and oh! Oh God! He was hard!

"I wanted...." Feebly, Skip rubbed at Richie's chest through his shirt. He wanted to take his *time*, dammit. This wasn't the car, this was his house, and it was *private* in here, and nobody was going to pound on the ceiling of the house and yell at them for kissing like faggots in Skipper's living room.

"Wanted what?" Richie asked, his lips parted just a little.

Oh... oh hell.

Skipper framed Richie's face with both hands, holding him, tilting him just so, and slanting his mouth over those full lips so he could—oh God, he just wanted to taste again.

Richie let out a charged groan of hunger, and Skipper thrust his tongue inside without thought. There was no *This is my buddy!* and no *Oh God, I'm kissing a man!*

There was only Richie—he tasted bitter, like tobacco, and hoppy like beer, but that wasn't what Skipper was really registering. All Skipper *really* registered was that he tasted like he smelled: salty and a little sweaty and a lot like soap and deodorant, because he'd obviously tried, just like Skipper had, to spiff up so they could kiss each other in Skipper's darkened house.

Richie had apparently spent his aggression on pinning Skipper to the door, because Skipper had the upper hand now, backing Richie into the living room proper, steering him around the coffee table, getting him to the couch. Richie sat down slowly, never breaking the kiss, his hands roaming under Skipper's shirt in a way that made Skipper absolutely crazy. Just touches, right? Midriff, back, chest— and touches had never really been Skip's thing. Usually the only thing that got Skip off was a hand directly on his cock, but Richie's hands could apparently make him hard by touching *anywhere*.

Oh my God! Especially his nipples.

Skip moaned and broke off from the kiss abruptly, burying his face against Richie's throat. "That's... *oh my fuckin' God!*"

Richie's laughter, low and helpless, made him feel a little better. Richie was captured too, lost as a butterfly in a hurricane. It wasn't just Skipper who couldn't stop but didn't know where they were going either.

"I'll do that again," Richie decided. "I like it when you groan like that."

Clever, pinching fingers found his nipple again and tugged. Skip arched and bucked and thrust—and bit the side of Richie's neck because he had nothing else to do.

23

Richie moaned just like Skip had, and for a moment, they were locked in a tug-of-war, Skip sucking a hickey on Richie's neck, Richie pulling on his nipple until he almost cried.

"I'm gonna come," Skip confessed. "Stop, I'm gonna—"

Richie wriggled out from under him and suddenly Skip found himself pinned to the couch. "You—your last girlfriend, that was Amber, right?"

Skip blinked several times, his body on such high alert that his brain had closed down words entirely. "Yeah."

"No girls between?"

"No...."

"You get health screenings?"

Screech! There went Skip's brain, doing a one-eighty on the wrong damned train track.

"What?" He pushed himself up on his elbows.

Richie rolled his eyes and started unbuckling the belt of Skip's slacks.

"I'm gonna suck your dick, okay? You don't got HIV or any shit like that?"

Skip's cock had a moment of gridlock. *Hurray! Richie's gonna put his mouth on me!* met *HIV or any shit like that?* head-on and vied for space. But Skip managed to get one thought out, and that let all the good stuff surge back in. "Negative. Last health screen, negative—oh God!"

Richie succeeded with his belt and slacks and Skip was exposed, cock slapping lightly on his lower abdomen, air cooling the dripping head.

"Oooh...." Richie paused for a moment just to look, and the breath from his gasp brushed the cap like a touch.

"Nungh!" Skip arched his hips off the couch and tried to spread his knees, but they were trapped.

"Kick off your shoes, Skip," Richie instructed, and when Skip was done with that, Richie shucked his pants, leaving him lying on his own couch, half-naked, still in his regulation maroon polo shirt.

24

"You too!" Skipper pushed himself up on his elbows again, wanting to see Richie naked. He *liked* Richie's body—even before he'd thought of Richie's lips, or his eyes in the moonlight, or the feel of his hands, Skip had liked Richie's body. Tight and stringy, muscular but not bulky. Not even a little—Richie had the body of a racing Chihuahua. Not big, no—but nobody would underestimate him, not in a fight, not on the soccer field, not—

Oh, oh yeah, right there, stripped naked, skin shining faintly in the light from the porch, slicked-back ginger hair wild about his head, boney-jawed face looking hungrily at Skip for approval.

"You like?" he asked, smiling nervously.

Skip reached out his hand. "Yeah. C'mere. Let me touch."

Richie leaned over the side of the couch, eyes still searching Skip's, and Skip made a realization. This... this was for real. Six years of playing soccer together, playing video games and watching movies, going out to beer and pizza with the guys—that had meant something to him and Richie.

This moment right here, skin-to-skin, this was scary.

Skip slid his hand along the back of Richie's neck, knotted his fingers in the ginger curls at his nape, and pulled him a little closer, close enough that Richie's breath fanned his face. "I like," he said simply, and if Richie's smile was a little wobbly, Skip couldn't blame him. He wasn't on solid ground either. The whole world trembled under the two of them, and the only time it felt right and solid was when they were close like this, close enough to touch.

Skip pushed up and took his mouth again, gentler this time, a sort of promise that he wasn't going to make fun of Richie's small stature or his red hair. Kids did that—*guys* did that. Skip caught hell for not having a beard, even after a week, for putting on five pounds if he wasn't careful, for having a slightly roman nose. He could take it. He was a big boy. But here, naked, new, Richie couldn't take it. Skip wouldn't dish it out. That wasn't fair.

Richie's body felt solid on top of Skip's, and their skin, oh Lord, *all of the skin* was touching. Oh, this was good—Skipper could do this all night. Keeping his fingers knotted in Richie's hair, he ravaged

Richie's mouth again and again and again. Richie whimpered and clutched his shoulders, bucking his hips against Skipper's, their cocks rubbing together, catching haphazardly, arousing, building, climbing to a pitch but not getting off—nope, not close. Just hanging there, suspended, in an agony of arousal.

Richie groaned and broke off the kiss.

"I promised," he graveled and then slid down Skipper's body, every ridge of muscle, every hair, every moist patch of skin catching on Skip's cock and his swollen testicles until Skip was ready to scream.

By the time Richie got to where he could grip Skip's cock and squeeze, Skip was incoherent, breathless, batting restlessly at Richie's head and shoulders while he tried to lock his mind around what he wanted.

"Sh...." Richie reached up and grasped one of his hands, lacing their fingers together, and Skip's frantic movements stilled. Richie's hand, practical and earthy, grounded him, and Skip squeezed tight and took a deep breath.

"Richie?" he whispered, not sure what he needed.

"Right here." Richie's breath brushed his cockhead, and Skip gasped.

"I'm...." A guy didn't say he was afraid. He didn't say that sex just got huge and unfathomable just because another man was touching him. But that's what was happening, and Skip knew that Richie's mouth on him would send him spiraling into a place he'd never imagined. "I'm...."

"Me too," Richie mumbled, and Skip relaxed. He didn't even know what Richie thought he'd been planning to say, but "me too" implied that they were in this together. Richie's evil little tongue darted out and licked the bell of Skip's cock, and Skip moaned. Together. They were in this togeth—

In one smooth movement, like he'd been practicing in his mind, Richie squeezed Skip's cock while stroking up and engulfed the head so he could suck.

The sound Skip made next came from some vital place inside him, the sensation so exquisite he felt tears start, and then forgot them.

Richie did it again and again and again, and Skipper arched his hips off the couch, thrusting into Richie's mouth, one hand gripping the cushion on the back of the couch and the other so tightly laced with Richie's fingers that his fingers grew cold.

For a moment Skipper tried to keep his eyes open, tried to keep his cool, tried to assimilate every feeling: the safety of Richie's hands, the sound of his own harsh breathing, even the slurping sounds of Richie's mouth enveloping Skipper's flesh.

That last one destroyed him. Richie was *sucking his cock*, and Skipper closed his eyes against the explosion of white lights behind them, against the convulsions of his body, the searing joy of his come....

The stupid tears seeping from under his eyelids and down his temples.

Finally Richie's mouth was too hard and Skip's cockhead too tender. He let out a pain sound and pushed Richie's head. "Done," he croaked, and Richie nodded and moaned, dropping his head to Skipper's thigh.

Fap fap fap fap fap.... Skip heard the sound, but for a moment he couldn't place it... and then Richie sucked in a mouthful of Skip's thigh and bit, his moan of orgasm loud enough to echo in the room.

Skip heard liquid hitting fabric and thought muzzily of the upholstery cleaner he had under the sink, and then Richie released his skin with a pop and moaned again, face buried against Skip's flank.

Skip let go of his hand and stroked his head comfortingly. That was the best part of sex, wasn't it? Someone there? Another person when the high of climax sent you spinning? Why else the laced fingers? Why else the kisses and the tenderness? Skip stroked those bronze curls with a shaking hand and then wanted more. He tangled his fingers in Richie's hair and tugged.

"C'mere," he rasped.

Richie pushed up and looked at Skip uncertainly. A shiny ring glazed the skin around Richie's lips, and his green eyes were lost and out to sea. "Uh—"

"Just lay on me," Skip said, trying for a smile. It was a plea. He wasn't sure if Richie knew it, but that's what he was doing.

Richie didn't ask, though. He sprawled on top of Skip, both of them naked and shivering. Richie buried his head in Skip's shoulder, his breaths sounding suspiciously close to sobs. Skip didn't hold it against him because the corners of his eyes still stung.

Skip reached up to the back of the couch and hauled the afghan he kept there down on top of Richie, to maybe warm them both.

Richie's shivers subsided, and it was just the two of them heating their little blanket fort against the chill.

"Skip?"

"Yeah?"

"That... you're not gonna... you know, call me a queer or anything."

Skip frowned in the darkness and went back to stroking his hair. "No," he said simply.

Richie pushed up and looked at him searchingly. "No?"

Skip shook his head, remembering Richie naked and a little vulnerable. "You... you're beautiful," he said, feeling foolish. "Wouldn't say anything to... you know. Make you feel like that was bad."

Richie's touch on his cheek was unexpected and tender. "It *was* good, wasn't it?" he asked, voice throbbing in wonder.

Skip nodded. "Yeah. That was...." He turned his head and kissed Richie's palm, tasting come but not sure whose. Skip licked a little and then turned back to Richie shyly. "That was real good, Richie. I... I've never had sex like that before."

Richie grinned like Skip had given him a big compliment, and then lay down flat against Skip's chest again. Skip pulled the blanket close around his shoulders, the better to keep him warm.

"You tired?" Richie asked, sounding puzzled.

28

"Actually, I got some cookies and milk," Skip told him. "Want to watch TV from my bed? We could huddle in the blankets 'cause it's warmer." He hadn't turned his thermostat on, and he needed to.

Richie's grin turned playful now, like a little kid's. "Won't we get in trouble for eating cookies and milk in bed?"

Skip grinned back and shook his head. "Not if we're the grown-ups," he said, feeling suddenly silly and joyous.

Richie lowered his mouth to Skip's and dropped a quick kiss. Skip opened his mouth and kissed back, and for a moment the kiss threatened to get bigger, but Skip suddenly wanted light and television and cookies and laughter, because getting bigger was going to take some strength.

He pulled back and nuzzled Richie's temple. "Good TV on tonight," he mumbled. "Let's watch that first. Then, you know...."

"Round two?" Richie said hopefully.

"Yeah."

That seemed to be all Richie needed. He pecked Skipper on the lips again and scooted off, letting the blanket slide with him.

Skipper stood up and wrapped it around Richie's shoulders, then put on his own underwear. "Go on and find something good," he said, turning Richie around and giving him a little shove. "I'll get us snacks."

His kitchen was small and unremarkable save for kitchen tile in a miserably heinous yellow/gold/lime green pattern that made most people want to vomit on sight. For some reason Skip wanted to avoid the inevitable discussion of barf in his kitchen—he wanted this to be nice.

He pulled out the box of cookies and paper towels and got a big cup of milk so they could share it.

But what if he doesn't want to share a big cup?

He just had my dick in his mouth—he's going to get picky now?

But people have preferences!

If he doesn't like it, he'll tell you. You can get him another glass.

I just want this to be....

29

What? Perfect? Different? What was he looking for from the man currently hunkering down under his comforter and channel surfing on his wall TV?

"Skip? Hurry up! I paused it, but they've already got to the part where the two guys bicker in the car. It's the best thing about the show!"

"Coming! Do you need your own cup for milk?"

"No—we can share."

Small things. Perfect things. How strange that the smallest things made the big thing, the unspoken thing, perfect.

"Lemon Oreos?" Richie asked when he got into his bedroom.

"I've got Chips Ahoy! if you want those instead." Skip said, taking his knee off the bed and replacing the coverlet. His bedclothes were browns and blues right down to the flannel sheets, and he was pretty sure it would hide the crumbs.

"No, no—they're just unusual."

"Yeah, well, I thought they'd be like the Girl Scout cookies—you know, the lemon ones?"

Richie made a little "oooh" shape with his lips, and Skip had to stop himself from just staring, fascinated. Those lips... they were soft and plump. How had Skip never noticed that those lips making that shape were....

His cock started to swell with blood underneath his boxers.

Yeah. They did that to him. Richie's lips, and the thought of what they had just done. Skip's hands were full or he would have had to stop and adjust himself. As it was, he balanced everything until he got into the bed, then handed Richie the milk and set the cookies between them.

Richie glanced at him casually and then caught sight of Skipper's semi falling out of his shorts, and leered. "That's awesome," he said bluntly. "What made that happen?"

Skipper's face heated. "Your mouth."

Richie flushed in blotches, and he pulled a cookie from the package with meticulous care. "That's, uhm...." He shoved the cookie in his mouth and then grinned at Skip with bulging cheeks.

Skipper laughed, not sure if he was *trying* to be dirty, but pretty sure he was trying to be funny about not knowing what to say. "Scoot over—they're about to blow shit up and that's my second-favorite part."

They situated themselves and Richie hit Play. Except for the fact that they were wearing their underwear and in bed, it was just like when Richie came over any other Friday night. Hazel hopped up and purred at the foot of the bed, and Skip and Richie sat shoulder to shoulder, commenting on the show.

"Hey, the little guy got to drive, didn't he?" Richie would say.

"Yeah—it sort of sucks that the other guy drives. It's his damned car."

"A power thing," Richie agreed, mouth full of cookie. "Big guy wants to have the biggest dick, so he gets to drive."

"Mm," Skipper disagreed. "'More'n that. See, the big guy, he's supposed to take care of things. He wants to take care of the little guy—it's how he's built."

"Little guy can take care of himself!" Richie laughed, sputtering crumbs, which he wiped off the comforter in a hurry.

Skipper rolled his eyes and offered Richie a napkin, which he took. "Yeah, but the big guy—it's not just cause he's big. He's like... you know. Special Forces. A commander. Everybody looks to him, and he's trying to take care of the little guy too. It's like me not letting Hazel out. That's not what she really wants. What she really wants is to stay here and crap in the cat box and get three squares a day. The little guy, he can take care of himself, but maybe he wants the big guy to protect him. He's had it sort of rough, you know?"

A commercial came on right then, and Richie paused it. "Rough how?" he asked.

Skip looked at the television. A woman was frozen there, showing off her scrawny ass in tight jeans, but Skip had never been interested in that kind of thing. "Uh... well... in the *show* he's had a divorce, and his wife hid her pregnancy, and you know this show. All family members are gonna get kidnapped or something."

31

Richie thought about that for a minute and then leaned in, their bare arms touching. He shifted his legs, and their calves tangled too. "And, uh, not on the show?"

Skip swallowed and stared at Richie's hand lying on the comforter between them. He reached out tentatively, like they hadn't just been naked and putting their mouths on places in the front room, and hadn't just come all over his couch. With one finger extended, he stroked the curve of Richie's thumb and forefinger, noting how still Richie held himself waiting for the touch.

"Maybe the little guy's family is sort of mean to him," Skipper said, thinking of the times he'd visited Richie at his parents' pick-n-pull but not wanting to intrude. Lots of shrill voices, people calling Richie small and weak and stupid. "Maybe the big guy just wants to not let that happen."

Richie closed his fist around Skipper's finger. "That's really... what's the word? Gallant. You're really damned gallant. But don't worry. Little guy, he can drive his own car, take care of himself. He's done it for years."

Skipper reclaimed his finger and covered Richie's hand with his own. "Yeah. Okay. Just know it's not always 'cause the big guy wants to have the bigger dick."

To his surprise, Richie leaned his head against Skipper's shoulder. "We already know you got the bigger dick, Skip. I know you don't got to prove anything."

Skipper's brain shorted out. He hadn't actually *seen* Richie's dick in the light, swollen and dripping, held tight in a fist. Suddenly he very much wanted to.

But Richie was *leaning against him*, and their hands were still touching. Skip took his cue from their moment together and laced fingers with Richie. Richie used his other hand to hit Play on the remote.

Their patter about the television show stilled, and it must have been the only thing keeping Richie awake, because before the show was done, Skip felt a gentle snoring against his shoulder.

He smiled a little. After checking that the milk glass was empty and safely stashed on the other end table, he set the rest of the cookies on the table closest to him. He turned off the light and the TV and stashed the remote, all without disturbing that gentle snoring.

Then carefully, very carefully, he slid down and rolled over to his side, nudging Richie until they were spooning, Skip's arm over Richie's chest.

"We were gonna do round two," Richie grumbled, and Skip nuzzled the back of his neck.

"We can do round two tomorrow," he reassured. "I'm not going anywhere."

"Good." Richie took Skip's hand and kissed it, leaving Skip stunned and breathless in the dark. "Don't know what I'd do without our Skip."

Your Skip, Richie. Team captain is sort of small compared to this right here.

But he didn't say it.

Richie was asleep, in his arms, in his bed. A week ago this was something he'd not even dreamed... okay, had he dreamed about it? In the dark, a new lover breathing against his chest, he had to ask himself if he'd ever dreamed about this.

I... I wanted his company. I wanted to look at him. I....

An image of Richie from that summer, running across the soccer pitch with his jersey held aloft in both hands, screaming in victory while the sun crisped his stringy body to a fine sweaty pink, crossed behind Skipper's eyes.

I really, really liked to look at—

Skip remembered that moment, felt in the pit of his stomach the urge to touch. They'd hugged and whooped and swatted each other's backsides, but had Skipper really....

I remember his hip bone pushing against my thigh. I wanted it harder. I wanted to hug him tight until all our skin was touching. I had to peel myself away, jump up and down, hug the other guys, because all I felt from them was sweat.

But not Richie. Richie had been special even then. Yeah, some of the guys came by Skip's place to watch Friday night television. Some of them had been over in the summer to help with the backyard. Some of them even asked if he had Halloween or Thanksgiving decorations up. But Richie knew it all. He knew what Skipper was doing over the weekend. He sent dumb YouTube videos over the week.

He knew about Skipper's mom.

This thing, this living breathing warm human thing, it had been brewing between them for a long time, hadn't it?

"Round two," Richie grumbled again, and Skipper hushed him and squeezed him tight enough that he'd be able to find himself.

"You won't lose me in the morning," Skipper whispered in wonder. It was true, because this moment here, this was not a sudden shot-in-the-dark, holy-crap-look-what-random-chance-made-us-do kind of thing. What lived between them hadn't changed overnight, *wouldn't* change overnight, because this heat, this live electricity passing from Skip's skin through to Richie and coming back again, this had been *building*. Six years before, the moment when Richie had looked up at Skip and said, "Yeah! Sure! Let's play rec league," had been the first layer of concrete that was them.

Or maybe the foundation had been laid before that, when Skip had wanted something, anything to impress his new friend in the dreary matter-of-factness of tech school.

This right here wouldn't go away. It breathed and murmured against Skip's chest, and sighed in his arms. It was him and Richie, as they always were, just a little more naked now.

Mornings After

IN A sitcom, they both would have awakened in the morning and been all freaked out about sleeping with a man, but sleep doesn't really work like that. In the middle of the night, Richie got up to go to the bathroom, and Skip rolled over to his other side. Richie spooned him, and they fell back asleep. A little closer to dawn, Skip did the same thing, and when he got back to bed, Richie was facing away, all ready to be spooned. Skip *couldn't* forget he was sleeping with Richie. Richie's smell permeated his dreams; the touch of his skin slid over Skip's body like silk, even in the deepest part of the night, when not even dreams disturbed unconsciousness.

In the morning Skip's eyes popped open and his hand immediately splayed over Richie's stomach, learning the feeling of each hard little ridge of muscle before his brain even screamed for coffee.

Richie *mmm*ed and rippled his body in a movement that was part stretch and part response. Skip's hand slipped lower, to the elastic of Richie's underwear, and he felt the bulge of Richie's cock against the cotton.

Without meaning to, Skip let out a long moan that shuddered through his body, and he mashed up tighter against Richie's back, nuzzling his neck and licking the edge of his shoulder. He traced that bulge with his thumbnail, thinking that it felt beautiful and warm and alive against his fingertips. His palm itched to hold it, to squeeze it, and when he thrust his hand under Richie's shorts to do just that, Richie let out a breathless little "Yesss" and arched into Skipper's grasp.

Oh…. Skipper's hips would not stay still.

That heat, the soft skin over it—he knew this feeling, had held his own cock in his hand when the mood struck him, but somehow Richie's was… better.

35

He grasped the base and stroked slowly up to the crown, and Richie leaned back against him, giving himself over completely to whatever Skip wanted to do. Skip wanted to touch first, to feel the incredible heat of Richie's shoulders against his bare chest under the covers. He wanted to rub his lips against Richie's ear and trace the edge, and whisper inside the whorl.

"That okay?"

"So good," Richie breathed.

"Want me to taste?"

Richie's noise then—raw and carnal and needy. He bucked his hips, and Skipper adjusted his grip so Richie's cock slid through.

He shifted position, scooting crossways on the bed in the same place Richie had been the night before, the blanket forming a forest green cocoon over his head.

Richie reached out, stroked Skip's backside through his shorts, ran his hand over Skip's flank. "Move," he begged throatily. "I want to touch—"

Skipper refused. Oh wow. There he was, eye to eye with the thing. He wanted to play, to taste, to learn what made Richie want, and he couldn't do that with the burn of Richie's touch on his body.

"My turn," he breathed, and even in the shadows of the blanket fort, he saw the spurt of precome as it washed over the head. It looked magical, and he stuck out his tongue to taste it.

Mm… bitter and earthy. Women were usually sweet. He'd never objected to a woman's taste, but it had never made him crave like that touch of magic on his palate. He flattened his tongue and licked the bell outright, enjoying the pound of Richie's hands through the comforter. More. He wanted more.

Skip covered his teeth with his lips and sucked Richie's cock until it bumped the top of his mouth.

No choking, not there, so he swallowed around the intrusion and stroked up some more. Oh Lord, this was *easy*. A leap like this, from having his dick sucked to having one in his mouth—it should have been frightening, but it wasn't. He wanted it. He *needed* it. He stroked his fist toward Richie's balls and sucked a little farther.

A sound tore from Richie's gut, and he ripped the covers away, leaving them in the sunlight, Skip's mouth full of cock. Skip pulled back, sucking the spit off as he went, and turned his head to the side, smiling shyly through what must have been a shiny glaze on his mouth. "Doesn't hurt, does it?"

Richie's eyes were enormous, and he shook his head no with a terrified reverence. "Feels great," he rasped. "You're gonna make me come—you sure you don't want to—"

"Look at you," Skip interrupted, because of course he wanted to, but he wanted to *do* for Richie this time. "Your cock is so pretty, Richie. It's *wide*—and pink. It's like a porn guy's cock, all straight and veiny." He grinned a little and licked up the vein on the back ridge like he was licking a line of ice cream off a cone.

Richie knotted his fingers in Skip's hair, the sting urging Skip on. "You... you like my cock?" Richie asked breathlessly.

Skip sucked it into his throat again, going a teeny bit farther than last time, then came up for air. "I like your whole body," he said, that shyness not leaving him alone. He ran happy fingers through the cinnamon trail that ran from Richie's navel to the curly patch at his groin. Richie's ass rose off the mattress like he couldn't control it, and it stayed a few inches off the mattress for a moment while Skip played.

Then Skip pulled him in again, this time moving his fist. He didn't go all the way down to the root, but since he was using his now free hand to fondle Richie's balls, he didn't reckon Richie would mind.

Richie's hips slammed down and thrust up again, and Skip wrapped his fingers around the base of Richie's cock—the better to stabilize it while Richie fucked his mouth.

Mouthfucked. Skull-dragged. Deepthroated.

Dirty words—*filthy* words—but Skip reveled in them. He was *doing* those things, and Richie was mumbling incoherently, begging him, urging him on, so he must have been doing them good.

Richie spread his legs, bent his knees, braced his feet against the mattress, and Skip found that he had access not just to Richie's balls but also to…. Oooh… the crease between his thighs, the cleft between his cheeks and beyond.

Everyone knew queers did anal—wasn't that what they were? *Queer.*

The word *queer* made his dick even harder than *mouthfucked.*

He thrust his head down hard on Richie's cock and slid his finger behind those big, baggy, furry balls. He barely brushed Richie's taint, barely slid back behind it and teased the indentation between his cheeks, when Richie cried out.

"Augh! Skip! Can't hold… gonna come. Gonna fuckin' *come!*"

Skip was ready.

Thick clots of it hit his teeth, his tongue, the back of his throat. He swallowed and sucked harder, letting Richie come straight down as he gulped. The bitterness didn't make him gag, and Richie's cock… oh, he could have sucked that down even farther, he was so in love with it.

Richie convulsed around him, knees coming up, arms wrapping around Skip's head.

"Sore, Skipper," he whispered, and Skip released him immediately, laying his head on Richie's stomach as Richie's extremities unraveled from the orgasm high.

Skip stared at Richie's face in wonder, undulating his hips against the mattress.

"Here," Richie said, nudging him up on all fours and scooting so his head was closer to Skipper's hips. Richie was obviously replete, because he just reached a hand under Skip while Skip stayed, still and vulnerable, his ass sticking out, his chin hovering directly over Richie's cock.

Richie caressed his backside slowly, making teasing little forays under Skip's stomach, and then he began to talk. "Like, I know we got a game, right, and we're going shopping afterward. But after the game, maybe… maybe I clean myself off real good and you… would you lick my asshole, Skip? The air, it felt real good, and I want you inside me… would that be okay?"

He punctuated the "okay" by wrapping his bony fist around Skipper's erection. Skip buried his face in Richie's thigh and thought about fucking Richie's asshole with his cock.

"That would be awesome," he whimpered, lips brushing the ginger hair at Richie's groin.

Richie laughed, low and dirty, and stroked him, playing with the precome on his dripping head.

That's all it took to make Skipper convulse and climax, collapsing facedown on the bed.

"Skip?" Richie whispered when Skip could hear something over his own heart.

"Yeah?"

Skip looked up and watched as Richie licked his fingers, the come running over them like ribbons. One finger at a time, he sucked Skip's ejaculate down, leaving them clean.

"Nungh...."

"Yeah," Richie said with satisfaction when he was done. He rested his damp hand in Skipper's hair, and for a moment they locked eyes, that held gaze the only speaking thing in the quiet of the sunlit room.

SKIP WOULD never remember moving after that, but they must have. He must have chivied Richie into the shower, because he cooked them both cheese eggs and toast, and he had a clear memory of Richie, hair wet around the collar of his nylon jersey, dropping eggs onto his clean shirt.

Skipper came forward, a damp paper towel in hand, and washed him off, and then Richie urged him into his own shower so they could hurry up and go lose the tournament game and go shopping.

They drove in Skip's car, and neither of them said a word about explaining why they'd do that. Richie had spent a lot of nights on Skip's couch—nobody would think anything of it.

But that didn't mean Skip didn't think about the world seeing them during the entire trip to the field. It must have been on Richie's mind, because as they pulled into the parking lot of Tempo Park, he looked at Skip in all seriousness and turned down his favorite Milky Chance song.

"Don't nobody need to know," he said quietly.

Skip swallowed and tried not to think about holding Richie's hand as they walked from the car, or of kissing him while swinging him around the field if they won. "I wouldn't mind—" he started hopefully, and Richie shook his head.

"Won't nobody play winter ball if they find out we're queer," he said matter-of-factly. "We both like playing. They don't need to know."

Skipper nodded, absurdly hurt. "No," he said. But then, low, between the seats, he turned his hand over so the back rested on the cup holder, and he looked at Richie with meaning.

Richie swallowed, his mouth twisting a little.

And then he rested his palm against Skipper's and laced their fingers together.

"We'll know," Richie whispered. "It'll be fine."

"Yeah."

Fine.

HE WORRIED, though, right up until he, Scoggins, and McAllister lined up on the pitch. As he and the team greeted, as he ran through the plays, as he assessed the other team during warm-up, he double-thought every time he patted someone's ass or flank or clapped them on the shoulder. Had he done the same thing to Scoggins, just as often? Had he done it less? Would anyone see it differently? Would they know? Could they tell, just by watching Scoggins scowl restlessly at the opposing team, that just hours before, Skipper had been sucking his thick red cock into his mouth and loving it?

Of course *that* line of thought was going to give him a boner, so maybe he'd better leave *that* bullshit alone!

But as soon as they lined up, moving their feet restlessly in the damp grass to keep their muscles from chilling, the breath from their heated bodies smoking faintly in the cold morning air, everything he and Richie had done in the past forty-eight hours went away.

It was his team, the ball, and the opposition, and God help anyone who got in their way.

Skip had expected to lose that first game, get ousted from the tournament, and then have the rest of the day—and Richie—to himself.

He didn't expect Scoggins to score the tie-breaking goal with a minute to spare, striking it so cleanly into the net that it cleaved the air between the goalie's fingers as he launched himself in for the intercept.

Skip didn't expect Scoggins and the team to be doing the victory dance, the cold forgotten, as McAllister lifted Scoggins up in the air on his shoulders and ran down the field.

He didn't expect to feel an evil knot of jealousy down in his stomach as he watched Richie Scoggins take a ride on another man.

Skip tamped down that feeling with a big stick and called the team to the sidelines to plan.

"I thought we were gonna lose," he said, and they all nodded at him soberly, because they had too. "How about we send someone to the store for more water and some dried fruit and shit, and we run some drills on the empty field down below this one. You all game?"

Scoggins grabbed Skip's keys and Skip pulled out his wallet to fund, but Scoggins waved him off. "You always buy, Skip—how 'bout the rest of these deadbeats pitch in!" He turned away then, avoiding Skip's eyes as he made the collection, but something in Skipper warmed.

The riding McAllister's shoulders? That was just regular playing stuff. But the collecting for the kitty? That was Richie having Skip's back.

That made playing *so* much easier the next time around. Skip pretty much forgot the entire queer thing and concentrated on playing.

And they won the *second* game too.

"Well shit," Skip muttered this time as they reconvened. Everyone looked at him in shock, and he grimaced good-naturedly. "Halloween's tomorrow, and I don't have any decorations! I gotta go buy them tonight, and I guess I'll put 'em up tomorrow after the game."

The guys were unimpressed.

The smile creases in the corner of Singh's eyes deepened as he squinted at Skipper in confusion. "We're actually *winning*, and you're mad because you can't *decorate?*"

Skipper shook his head. Oh no. This was going to be a thing, wasn't it?

Jefferson shook his head. "Man, you got just enough time. What is it, three? Yeah—you and Scoggins run and buy shit now, and you might have some time for setup before it gets too dark. You don't want to have Halloween without stuff up, and candy and shit. Kids will *destroy* you if you're not prepared."

Skipper grinned at him. Jefferson still lived with his mother—mostly so he could support her—but even without that, he was such a good egg.

"*That's* what I'm talking about. Okay, guys, don't forget tomorrow is 'fall back.' Set your clocks before you go to bed or you're gonna be *real* pissed off when you get in early and nobody's here to practice."

"Oh my God!" Galvan and Owens were practically in stereo. "God, thanks, Skip—way to have our backs!"

With that the team broke up, leaving Skip and Scoggins to haul ass up the hill, sweaty under their hooded sweatshirts but chilling quick in the October wind.

And then, right *then*, as they were hustling their asses to Skip's car, was when Skip missed it. The wind was whipping at their faces, and they'd just won two games, and they were going to go do something *fun* with their weekend, and *damn* if Skip didn't want to hold Richie's hand.

He contented himself with what they would do later, after decorations, and dinner, and cookies, and TV, when it was him and Richie, breathing alone together in the dark.

"HEY, SKIP!" Richie said playfully, pointing to the creepy dolls, artfully shattered and de-haired and staring into space with blank glass eyes through masks of fake blood. "Let's get a bunch of those and hang them from your tree!"

Skip stared at the macabre decoration and grimaced. "That's a shitload of money, Richie—I still gotta decorate for Thanksgiving, and I've got about *three* ornaments for Christmas. Maybe we—"

"Ooh! I got it!" Richie started bouncing up and down on his toes. "Okay—you get the tombstones and the strobe light and the ghost thing and shit. I'll be right back. I'm going to the dollar store—it's one store over, okay?"

Skip nodded, bemused, and Richie took off, his feet flapping on the ground like he was eleven instead of twenty-five. God, that sort of enthusiasm was contagious.

Skipper bought his decorations—and threw in a giant spiderweb and a Frankenstein mask for kicks—and when he was done, Richie was standing outside with a bag of cheap plastic Barbies, red paint, and rough jute twine.

"Isn't it great!" he crowed. "It cost me about twenty bucks—that's what *one* of those things cost in that specialty store. C'mon, I want to get this shit up before it's dark. We need a trial run."

"But I didn't get candy!" Skip complained. "I need to have the candy, or all this decoration is gonna be moot, because the little bastards will *destroy* my yard!"

The year before, he'd had to relive his least favorite memories from growing up, and turn off all the lights and pretend not to be home.

"Well, you have to go get a pumpkin anyway. Drop me off home and run and get candy, and you'll have it all ready for tomorrow night after the game. How's that?"

Skip nodded, relieved. It was probably silly, a grown man making such a big deal out of this, but he hadn't had a house with decorations and candy and a porch light and… and *normalcy* since before his parents' divorce.

Suddenly this holiday loomed up, and he had a friend who would help him make it perfect, and not in a sad, lonely way either. Hanging the dolls from his little tree in the front yard was a stroke of genius—kids would love it (or hate it) and it would be…

Happy. He'd give the big honkin' candy bars, and kids would walk away thinking that yeah, that guy in the little house with the brick bottom and the stucco was an all right guy.

It was something he hadn't had as a kid, and he was starting to realize—like just this moment, watching Richie get all excited *like* a kid—how much memories like this meant to him.

He was so glad Richie was there to share them with.

BY THE time it was dark, they'd managed to hang all the creepy plastic dolls from the tree and suspend the ghost and the strobe light on the front of the porch. They were both starving, so Skip sent out for pizza, and it arrived while Richie was practically armpit deep in the giant pumpkin Skip had bought when he'd been getting candy.

They took turns eating and working on the jack-o'-lantern, and when they were done, Skip surveyed it with critical eyes.

"Hunh… your parts are real good, Richie, but I think I mangled that… whatever it is, filigree, around the outside edge."

They'd gone for one of the more difficult pictures in the carving kit, and there was this weird twisty vine thing surrounding the witch over the cauldron. Skip was actually convinced the whole thing was overkill—as far as he was concerned, jack-o'-lanterns should have big goofy faces on them with triangular eyes, like in the cheap clipart, but Richie had insisted. The *good* ones used the books and perforated the pumpkin on the lines and then carved the detail pieces out with the tiny serrated knives that came with the kit. Skip wasn't going to argue with him about it—he just shut up and carved the damned filigree.

Richie stood back next to him, munching on pizza and studying the work critically. "No, no. I think you did real good for your first time." He stopped chewing and swallowed abruptly. "Why was it your first time carving a pumpkin, Skip?"

Skip shrugged and stepped forward to wipe the face off so the last of the inside mung didn't obscure the picture. "I was, like, ten when my parents split. Who puts a butcher's knife in the hands of a ten-year-old?"

44

"Yeah, but after that? I mean…." Skip looked over his shoulder and caught Richie frowning at him. "I know your mom was… like queen of vodka and shit, but didn't you get to carve a pumpkin?"

"No," Skip said shortly, not wanting to talk about it. Richie looked hurt, and Skip sighed. "She got welfare and child support, and once I paid the rent and bought food, there wasn't much left. I mean, *now* I know about those cheap places to shop and the dollar store and shit, but back then I didn't have a car and the closest grocery store wasn't cheap."

"But…." Richie looked at him, baffled. "Skip, you were just a kid. I mean, my folks split up too—and I can't say my stepmom's a picnic. But you were just a *kid.*"

Skip shrugged again, uncomfortable. "Well," he said, "I must not have done *all* the shopping. I still barely look old enough to buy vodka."

Richie set his pizza crust down deliberately on top of the box and wiped off his hands. Then he slid behind Skipper and wrapped his arms around his waist and held him hard.

It took a moment for Skip to recognize comfort.

He turned in Richie's arms and captured his chin, then went in for a kiss. Richie smiled a little right before their lips brushed. "Are you sure? I taste like—"

Pepperoni and sauce.

Didn't matter.

This kiss seemed different. They were both still sweaty with two soccer games and running around decorating, and still covered in pumpkin guts. Richie even had a seed stuck to his forearm. They weren't heading for bed—at least *Skip* didn't want to have sex like this, not tonight. It was just… warm. It lingered, the purpose of the kiss being the kiss itself.

Richie pulled away first and gave a shuddering sigh, pushing against Skipper and letting out a little puppy-dog sound. "Let's clean up and shower," he said gruffly. "We can skip the cookies in bed—I just want you."

"Yeah." They were tired. Not *bone-deep* tired, because Skip knew he was still ready to go, but if they had that kind of kiss in bed, one of them would fall asleep in the middle.

Skip had *plans* for tonight.

"You go first," he said decisively. "I'll finish cleaning up."

TWENTY MINUTES later he stepped out of the shower in his tiny bathroom, wondering if he should even bother to put on underwear. Being naked under the pulsing water made him remember that morning, the look on Richie's face, the taste of his come in Skip's mouth, and he wanted *more*.

He was still drying his hair with one towel and clutching the other towel around his hips when he stepped into the bedroom and saw Richie sprawled out naked on the bed with his cock in one hand and a bottle of lubricant in the other.

Skip promptly dropped both towels. "You, uh… were we…."

Richie looked up at him with hooded eyes. "I really…." He set the lube down and let go of his cock so he could sit up. "It's not supposed to hurt," he said after a moment. "It's… it's supposed to feel really good." Richie lay back then and lifted his legs, reached behind him, and spread his cheeks. "See?" he said huskily. "Right there."

Skip closed his eyes, gripped his own cock, and squeezed a drop of precome out the tip, shuddering. "I know where your asshole is, Richie," he said, not sure he recognized his own voice. "I'm not just gonna stick it in."

Richie dropped his legs and pushed himself up on his elbows, grinning. "But you *are* gonna stick it in, right?" he said slyly.

Skipper let go of his cock and smiled self-consciously. "You want?"

Richie nodded, and Skip reached over and killed his bedside light.

Richie's eyes got big and shiny. "You don't like looking at me?"

Skipper bit his lip. "Just, you know, worried you don't like looking at *me*."

Richie shook his head and held out his hand in a curiously hopeful gesture. "I *really* like looking at you. I... I can't look *away* from you sometimes."

Skip took his hand and bounded into bed, eager as a puppy. "Right? Like all summer, I kept waiting for you to take off your shirt, and you'd be all sexy and sweaty and shit. It was why I wanted to win!"

Richie chuckled. "You never take off your shirt, you miserable bastard." He ran a hand over Skip's chest, stopping to brush his thumb against a pink nipple. "Why is that?"

Skip's face heated, and not just because the caress was like a little pleasure dart straight to his balls. "'M fat," he mumbled.

Richie squinted at him. "Not hardly!" He scooted to the side and pulled a mouthful of Skip's stomach skin into his mouth.

"Nungh!" Oh God, that felt good too! But Richie was playing with his muscle ridges and his nipples and the cuts of abdomen underneath his hip bones.

"It's a four-pack and not a twelve-pack, man, but not fat!"

Skip wiggled in sheer arousal. "I... you know. Fat kid... doesn't go away."

Richie cocked his head again, like a spaniel listening for unheard signals. "You weren't fat," he said, voice quiet. "You showed me pictures once."

The one picture of his family happy. The other picture of him in his senior year of high school, paid for with his after-school job so he wouldn't be completely invisible in the yearbook. The first picture full of fake smiles and carefully ironed collars, and the second replete with baby fat and acne.

"You know, 'Mama's own little fat boy.'" He tried to keep the bitterness out of his voice when he did an imitation of his mother.

Richie stopped playing with his stomach, which was too bad because he'd just gotten to the part where Skip's cock lay, dripping, begging for attention.

"You're...." Richie ran his hands down Skip's thighs, up his torso, and stopped, framing his face with those work-roughened, bony hands. "Just like you said to me last night, Christopher. You're beautiful. *You* are… I could touch you all night, but it makes me want."

Skip fumbled for words and Richie took pity on him, moving down and engulfing his cock in one fast suck. For a few wonderful, oblivious moments, there was only that edgy heat, the pressure of Richie's lips, Skip's moans echoing in the dark behind his eyes.

"Look at me." Richie's breath teased his cockhead, and Skip had no choice.

"You're so fuckin'… fuckin' *hot* right now." Richie scrambled to his knees and grabbed the lube from under the pillow.

Richie bent over on all fours and squirted some lube on his fingers and fumbled for his hole.

"Wait!" Skip sat up and stopped him, not wanting the touching to be over. "Just… slower, Richie." He bent over Richie's backside and placed little fluttering kisses down his freckled spine. Richie gasped, and Skip went firmer against his ribs. The taut, stringy muscles of Richie's stomach contracted under Skip's hands as he ran them up and down Richie's front and his chest. By the time he got to Richie's bottom—avoiding the patches of lube as he went—Richie was emitting a steady keening moan.

Skip parted his cheeks and looked. The pink little pucker squeezed and released as he watched, and he thought, *My dick is not going to fit there.*

He'd had a girlfriend who liked this, though, and she'd been shameless, showing him how to stretch her, how to make sure he didn't hurt when he went in. He'd liked her—he'd liked her a *lot*—but with every burning frisson of Richie's skin against his own, he was starting to suspect why they were never able to pass "like" into "love."

He spread Richie's ass a little wider and licked.

Clean—it tasted a *lot* like Skip's soap, actually, and Skip spat three or four times so he wouldn't get sick on amber bodywash. Then he licked again, like he meant it, and Richie moaned deeper and buried his head in the pillow in front of him. Skip licked more, and harder, his interest in the sounds Richie made, the way his thigh muscles trembled, the incoherent little pleas he was screaming into the pillow, *far* outweighing any discomfort because of taste. Oh wow—look at what he was doing to Richie!

Richie started to rock back and forth, begging him, not for anything specific, just "Please... oh God, Skip, please!"

Skip pulled back enough to test the rim with his finger, and Richie gasped and thrust against him, taking Skip to the second knuckle. Skip added another finger and twisted, stretching, not just to hear Richie gibber (although that was fun too) but to make sure.

He didn't want to hurt his friend.

"Here, Richie—gimme the lube."

He oiled himself up generously, making sure the lube was skin temperature before he placed his cock where he needed to go.

Richie groaned and pushed back, taking him in one solid gulp, and Skipper's vision went dark.

Oh my God. Oh my God. I'm assfucking Richie Scoggins and I want him... I want him... oh fuck I want him so fucking baaaaaad....

Richie was rocking back and forth, keening, and Skip suddenly took over. He placed his hand firmly on Richie's lower back and started his own rhythm, feeling the drag of Richie's sphincter as he pulled out almost to the crown and the push of it as he thrust back in. Thrust and pull, thrust and pull, every stroke along his nerve endings like fireworks.

"Oh God.... Skip, it's like... like fuckin'... so...."

"Magic," Skip whispered hoarsely, and then he slammed his hips forward *hard*, because if Richie had words, he was doing better than Skip.

"*Yes!*" Richie howled, and Skip did it again, and again, hard and staccato, every smack like a scream of pleasure from his crown to his balls to his own asshole.

"Fucking you!" he gasped.

"Yeah! Fucking me!"

"So hard!"

"Fucking hard!"

"So good...." Skip's voice caught, and something in him broke. "So fucking good, Richie!" *Why weren't we doing this six years ago?*

"*Don't stop!*" Richie howled, and Skip kept on going. Again, and again, faster, until the drag of Richie's skin was almost numbing, until....

"*Augh! Yes! There!*"

Skip pulled out slowly and tried to hit that spot again.

And one more time.

And....

Richie buried his face in the pillow and screamed, his entire body convulsing around Skip's cock, clasping him in the slick-fisted vise of his body.

In the sudden silence, Skip could hear Richie's breathless moan, and then that sound again, of a spoonful of tapioca flung at a canvas sail.

Skip's vision darkened and he came, huge, dumping what felt to be a lifetime of spend into Richie, marking him from the inside out as irrevocably Skip's now, nobody else's. Skip was *this* kind of friend, and nobody else could be.

Richie collapsed under him and Skip fell over his back, both of them flat in the yellow light from the bed stand, trying to see again, trying to catch up to the now.

Richie groaned and Skip tried to remember how to move. "'M I crushing you?"

"No. Don't want you to leave me."

"Not gonna leave," Skip mumbled. "May have to pull *out*, but I'll be right here."

"That feel as good for you as it did for me?"

"God, yeah. You, uh... wanna try it on me someday?"

Richie went still. "Not soon," he said, voice shaky. "I knew you wouldn't hurt me, Skip. Not so sure about me not hurting you."

Skip grunted and lazily licked the sweat off the back of Richie's neck. He slid sideways, feeling the come that dribbled when he pulled out. He pulled the comforter over their cooling bodies and ignored the fact that they were both naked. They'd wake up and pee, and probably put on their shorts then.

Right now he turned off the bed stand light and snuggled down, Richie replete and exhausted in his arms. A furry body thumped on the bed, and he felt the familiar weight of Hazel picking her spot down by his toes.

Oh Lord. It was fall back. His phone was set on the bed stand, and it would ring a whole hour later than it had rung this morning.

And he'd wake up again with Richie snug and sexy in his bed.

SKIP HAD never given himself credit for any sort of imagination. He could get soccer plays from books, but he didn't make up any of his own. He could fix computers, but he had no urge to write his own code or design his own hardware or software. But he did read—mostly thrillers and espionage, because he liked to see if they got the tech things right.

He read enough, watched enough movies, to be able to envision a perfect day.

That Halloween Sunday was a perfect day.

He woke up with Richie in his arms, and that was a start. They didn't have enough time to fool around, but they did kiss, long and slow, like they'd *always* wake up in the same bed, like they'd *always* have time for sex, like they'd *always* be in each other's arms.

They took turns in the shower, and this time, when he got out, Richie had made coffee. They ate cold pizza for breakfast (because *cold pizza*!) and were out to the field half an hour early for warm-up. The smell of cold, of wood smoke, and the midautumn haze—all of it sang in Skipper's bones. It wouldn't matter if they won or lost—he was playing soccer with his friends, with someone who cared about him, and yes, damn, he finally knew what sex was about.

And then they won the game.

This time *he* was the one who lifted Scoggins on his shoulders and ran with him down the field. In six years of that soccer club, three seasons a year, they hadn't taken the championship once.

51

Running down that field, Scoggins whooping with his arms out under the heartbreak blue of the Halloween sun, felt like flying.

That night Richie hid behind the tree and waited for the older kids to walk up to the front porch. As soon as the motion sensor kicked on for the ghost, Richie popped out from behind the tree wearing the Frankenstein mask, roaring, and the brave kids who got past *that* got the candy bars.

One tiny little girl slipped by Richie's radar, but when he jumped out and hollered, she squealed, "Do it again! Do it again!" so it wasn't too bad after all. (Skipper liked that kid—he gave her extra chocolate, and she gave it to her little brother, who was sitting down at the sidewalk in a stroller.)

When Richie got tired of that, he answered the door and roared, and Skipper handed out the candy bars anyway, but that didn't last long. Richie needed to be active, and apparently chasing kids was its own awesome sport.

One mom with zombie makeup and a blood-soaked pink bathrobe laughed appreciatively as she balanced a squirming little zombie on her hip.

"Your boyfriend's really good with kids," she said, laughing, and she turned away with her wiggling kid before Skipper could reply.

What would he say? That Richie wasn't his boyfriend? That they weren't "that" way? Because they *were* that way, and Skipper wouldn't mind if they were boyfriends.

But what? He was just going to bring that up? Stop Richie as he chased some high school kids through Skipper's yard and tell him, "Hey, I think you and me, it's more than a weekend thing or some fucking when you're staying over for video games. It's real. We're boyfriends. Is that okay?"

Richie trotted back up to the porch, still laughing as he tore the mask off his face. "I think I put the fear of God in those little bastards!" he crowed. "They're not coming back for a triple helping of candy—not on *my* watch!"

Skip wanted to laugh with him—he did! But all he could think was *I want to kiss him! I want to throw my arm over his shoulder and ask him if he wants a triple helping of candy, and hear him laugh dirty! I want—*

"Skip, anything wrong?" Richie asked. Skipper fumbled for words and Richie started going through the candy bowl in his arms. "Oh, hey! You still got *massive* quantities of Almond Joy—excellent! Those are my favorites!"

Skip said, "Yeah, I got lots left over. It's nine o'clock—you think anyone else is coming by?"

Richie looked out into the gentle little neighborhood. Most of the porch lights were still on, and they could see flocks of children moving like starlings from porch to porch. "I'd say wait until ten." He yawned. "I'll be ready to go to bed by then anyway." He leered up at Skip. "Gotta get my fun in before the weekend's over, you know?"

Skip nodded unhappily. He thought about saying it, then decided against it and was completely horrified when it came out of his mouth anyway:

"I wish you didn't have to go home."

Richie didn't look horrified—he looked sad.

"Yeah, me too." They'd locked Hazel in the bathroom, so they were standing in a lighted doorway. The whole world could see them. And Richie grinned up at him and tapped his cheek gently with a knuckle. "You think I want to leave a place that serves cold pizza for breakfast and has Almond Joys?"

Skip rolled his eyes and grinned, and they went back inside to watch *Insidious: Chapter 3* before the next round of kids came by

Naked Limbs and Fallen Leaves

THAT NIGHT they did the thing again, but something was different. It was like they'd gotten some of the "Right the fuck now!" out of the way and they could go slower. Skipper was gentle with Richie when he knew Richie was about to come, pulling back and letting Richie's cock flop out of his mouth and cool in the air. Richie drew Skipper's blow job out a little, slowing down when Skipper warned him, and moved so Skip could stroke him off while Richie was deepthroating Skip.

They turned off the lights this time, because both of them were tired, and Richie said he'd eaten too much chocolate to do the butt thing. It didn't matter. The sexual contact, the explosion of orgasm behind Skip's eyes, Richie's little whimper as he buried his face in Skip's thigh—all of it made for the perfect day.

But the next day they had to get up early. Their morning was a flurried game of "I got next!" in Skip's tiny bathroom. One of them shaved while the other one shit, and one of them showered while the other one shaved. They ended up dressing at the same time, Skip in his polo shirt and tan pants, Richie in his mechanic's blues and jeans.

Skip shoved toast in Richie's hand before they both ran out the door. Richie paused, one hand on the doorknob, his duffel bag over the other shoulder, and Skip grabbed his lapels suddenly and hauled him in for a thorough, lip-pulping, cock-hardening, nipple-tightening mauling. When Skip released him, Richie let go of the doorknob to rub his lips.

"What was that for?" he asked in wonder.

Skip was already hot from the kiss, but he knew his face got even redder. "Just... don't forget this weekend, 'kay? Was... you know. Like the best weekend in my life. Want another one."

Richie's smile was almost shy. "You want another one?"

Skipper bit his lip. "That okay?"

"Yeah. I mean...." A smile of wonder split Richie's face. "*Yeah!*" He reached behind Skip's neck and hauled him down for another kiss, and this time Skipper found himself smiling when it was done. "We're gonna do it again, right?" Richie asked, their faces so close Skip could feel little puffs of Richie's breath across his lips.

"Next weekend," Skip promised rashly. "We'll go out to a movie Friday, play Saturday—can't promise we'll win—"

"Who cares!" Richie said, clearly enchanted. "Friday! I've got a reason to survive the fucking week now! That's *awesome!*"

He was out the door before Skip could tell him that he could come by *any* day. *Any* day was a day Richie could hang out on his couch, play his video games, strip naked, and molest Skip's unprotesting body.

But it didn't matter, because they were going to do something on Friday. Richie would find his way to Skip's door when he needed to, right?

BY LUNCHTIME, Skip was staring at his phone like it had the secret of the universe.

"Skip," Carpenter muttered, "you're up!"

Skip looked at the phone bank, swore, ignored his cell phone, picked up his work line, and squeezed his squishy brain-shaped toy. "Tesko Tech Business Services! This is Skipper, how can I help you?"

"Oh, hey! Skipper! My boy! Lucky me, I got you again!"

Oh Lord. Skipper rolled his eyes at Carpenter and mouthed, "Mr. Gay Porn." Carpenter made an obscene gesture using his fist and his closed mouth and his tongue in his cheek.

Skipper grinned and walked Mr. Gay Porn through his paces. When he was done, the guy laughed and said, "We're going to have to stop meeting like this, Skipper. Any chance we can meet any other way?"

Oh boy. Skipper sighed grimly. "Actually, I'm seeing someone right now, sir. And this is highly inappropriate."

"Oh...." That sound was not promising, in that it didn't sound like Mr. Gay Porn would go away. In fact, that sound was highly *un*promising. "You are seeing some*one*. You didn't say a *girl*. You said you are seeing some*one*. I find that interesting. Don't you find that interesting?"

Skipper pasted a smile on his face. "Thank you, sir, for using the tech services at Tesko. If you have any questions or any complaints about the service you've just received, feel free to dial the number provided by your employee manual. Thank you again, and have a nice day!" He hung up. "Without *me*," he finished with passion.

"What's the matter, Skipper? He having trouble realizing that no means no?"

Skipper turned to his friend and shook his head. "Man, you'd think the guy would... I don't know. Take the hint. I told him I was seeing someone—"

"You are?" Carpenter took a deep drag from his flavored water and looked eager. "Tell me more!"

Skipper blinked. "You act like I haven't ever dated before!"

Carpenter rolled his eyes and took another drag. "Skipper, my last girlfriend was a year ago. She was sweet, didn't mind that I was fat, and left me because her old boyfriend came back and she loved him more. It was very sad. *Your* last girlfriend was Amber. You broke up for unspecified reasons, about *five months before* Trisha and I broke up. The fact that you've been seeing someone is a big deal. C'mon, man—you're my only friend who doesn't practically live online— hook me up with some real-life details!"

For a moment Skipper wanted more than anything to tell him about Richie. Carpenter *loved* liberal political causes. If Skipper was a betting man, he'd put down actual money that the fact that his love life had magically changed from an "Amber" to a "Richie" wouldn't do more than surprise him.

But... but *Richie* hadn't said it was okay, and that held him back. Richie had said they'd see each other over the weekend, but that wasn't a confession of... of commitment or anything.

It was just "Hey, man, what're you doing next weekend?" "Well, I thought we'd try that fucking thing again, what do you think?" "Fucking sounds great, Skip—how about fuck my ass again!"

Richie and Carpenter saw each other all the time. They liked each other. Skip *couldn't* tell Carpenter about the... the new thing, the fucking thing, because that just wouldn't be fair.

Skip looked at his phone again, longingly. It would be so much easier if he and Richie could just *text*, the way Amber used to text him. Stupid shit—catching up on your day sort of shit.

Actually....

"How do you know when you're okay to text someone?" he asked Carpenter thoughtfully. "I mean, is there an etiquette or something?"

Carpenter scratched at the scruff on his cheeks. "I don't know. Are you going to see this person again?"

Skip smiled, thinking of how excited Richie had been. "Yeah, this weekend. You know, uh, after the game." And before the game, and God, wouldn't it be great if they could see each other after practice as well?

"Wow—you found someone who would work around your obsession with soccer!" Carpenter let out a low whistle. "This is serious. You've ditched many a LAN party for soccer, my friend."

Skip rolled his eyes and checked his call light. So far it had been pretty low-key, and they were getting close to lunch. "C'mon, let's go walk to that deli on the corner," he said, hitting his break signal and gesturing for Carpenter to do the same. "And you know, you could play too. It'd be good for you."

Carpenter paused in the act of hitting his break signal. "I must have had too much coffee this morning. I could have sworn you just said I could play on your precious soccer team."

Skip shrugged and Carpenter hit the signal anyway. "Why not? It's rec league, man—nobody's in it for the blood, you know?"

Carpenter rolled his eyes. "Yeah, I suppose the fact that I'm a fat asshole who cannot *possibly* haul this piece of meat down the field has totally escaped your notice."

Skip frowned and together they trotted out of the building toward the sandwich place at a decent clip. Apparently November had called a halt to the shiny, blustery days of fall and ushered in the low-hanging fog and dank days of the season. Ah, well, it meant that Skip's run after work that evening would be a little more pleasant.

"Look, since it's winter ball, we do running and drills on Thursday night. Show up for practice and learn some of the plays. I'll bring some of my old gear—it'll fit. We've only got one sub this season—just having someone to sub for the defenders would be great. You can be the guy who hangs out in front of the goalie and just keeps the box clear."

Carpenter grunted, but he was keeping up with Skip and Skip wasn't going slow. "Are they gonna hate me if I lose the game for them?"

Skip remembered the time he'd kicked the ball into the goal and it had bounced off the post and halfway downfield. In a stroke of luck, the opposing team's midfield had trapped it midbounce and kicked it into the Scorpions' goal for the win. The team—mostly the same guys—had laughed all the way off the field.

"Naw, man," Skip said sincerely. "We wouldn't have lasted this long if they were all douchey and shit."

Carpenter puffed, blowing slightly, and slowed down as they approached the deli. "Yeah," he panted. "Why not. God knows more exercise couldn't hurt."

Skip grinned, happy both on the count of distracting Carpenter and because *now* he had something real and not annoying and not clingy to text Richie about.

He pulled his phone out of his pocket while they were in line and was surprised to see Richie's text box open.

Hey. How's your day?

Sweet! It felt like the clouds and the fog had parted and the sun had spilled down on Carmichael after all.

Not bad. Convinced Carpenter to do drills with us Thursday and maybe sub on Saturday.

:(

The emoji caught Skip by surprise.

I thought we had plans on Saturday.

Well I told him I had a date afterward. He won't be expecting me to hang around.

:) *Good. I'm glad I get to be your date.*

:) *Me too. But Carpenter is okay, right?*

As long as he's not spending the night at any time during the weekend, life is all good.

Skip had to make his order then, so he signed off, and he and Carpenter talked during lunch about what drills he'd be best at.

But at the end of lunch, as they were walking back—a little slower, because they were both a little full—Carpenter changed the subject.

"So who were you texting, you know, when we were in line?"

Skip was proud—he didn't flush, he didn't fluster, and hell, his heartbeat didn't hardly speed up. "Richie—just double-checking about you playing on the team. He said yeah, that's fine."

"Hm," Carpenter mumbled, almost to himself. "Okay. Glad to know you cleared it with your boy."

"Yeah, well, you know. Richie's good people. He's happy you're on board."

He didn't hear Carpenter's reply, and it was just as well. They were a little late back from their break, and they had to hustle to their cubicles or they'd get in trouble. That was fine, though—hustling Carpenter to the sandwich place for the exercise had been Skip's principle motivation in going. Skip didn't have many people in his life. He liked to keep everybody healthy.

THAT NIGHT Skip found another excuse to text Richie—something about Hazel missing him—and they had a good half-hour conversation. The next morning he woke up to find a smiling, sleepy-eyed picture on his phone—Richie's wake-up pic. Skip returned the favor, and Richie's next pic wasn't nearly so family friendly.

OH MY GOD!

What? You saw it before!

Not on my phone! Jesus, it scared me. Looking at me with its one big eye!

HAHAHAHAHAHAHAHA

You laugh, but I've been dreaming about that thing. Having it show up on my phone was a little too real.

Not real enough, though, because I'm not there!

Skip sighed. *How about you stay Thursday night too?*

I wish. My stepmom's setting me up with a family friend. I've got to go pretend that's a possibility.

Skip almost dropped the phone.

Skip?

Skip you there?

His phone rang, and this time he *did* drop it. By the time he recovered, Richie was in midramble.

"Skip, I'm not gonna *date* her. I just—Kay set this up and we're just all eating dinner after soccer practice, okay?"

Skip took a deep breath. "I don't want you dating anybody else," he said shortly, feeling that jealousy rising again. "I... I mean, I get your stepmom doesn't know, and you don't want to tell her—"

"Not while I'm still living here," Richie said hurriedly, and Skip took another deep breath. Richie had been saving to move out from his parents' garage loft for the past year. It didn't help that his parents charged standard rent to their own son, but he was getting it done.

"So... after you move out?" Skip asked, feeling pathetic.

"Yeah, Skip. If you and me... I mean... you know. Right now it's just this weekend."

The third deep breath must have been the charm, because Skip calmed down.

"Yeah," he said, feeling his heartbeat slow. "Sorry. Didn't mean to go all psycho on you."

"No," Richie said softly. "Not psycho. You just wanted to know... wanted to know where we are, that's all."

"Yeah," Skip said, not sure if they had a better idea now or not.

"How's this," Richie said, sounding practical. "I *liked* how we didn't have to worry about rubbers. I think we should stay in that place. Does that work for you?"

"Yeah, okay." Because that was a good place. Even Skip knew that. "I can deal."

"Good. Now bail, or we're both gonna be late for work."

"'Kay. Bye, Richie. See ya Thursday."

"See ya Thursday."

Skip hung up and got in the shower feeling particularly unsatisfied. See you Thursday? When they weren't going to spend any time alone together?

Well where was the fun in that?

Still, it didn't stop them from texting every day—and it didn't stop Skip's heart from glowing like an amber autumn sun when he saw Richie's name lit up on his phone.

THURSDAY WAS pure torture, in its way.

On the one hand, the team was *awesome* with Carpenter. They gave him some drills and some things to work on at home, and they worked on a rotation schedule, so Carpenter could spell one of the defenders, and then the defenders could go out and spell the midfielders or the strikers. It wasn't a perfect system—people might only get three minutes to catch their breath in the half—but it sure did beat what they had in place now, which was nothing, because they had just the bare amount to play.

McAllister, being the big, hulking Irishman that he was, seemed to have taken Carpenter under his wing, but not entirely in a good way.

"Pushy bastard," Clay muttered under his breath after McAllister painstakingly explained a play that pretty much any kid out of the under-eight leagues would get.

But Jefferson heard him and rounded in on Mac. "You know, he's big, he's not brain-dead. I'm sure he's got the play down by now, okay?"

McAllister rolled his eyes and turned his back, and Skip knew that was the best they'd get out of the guy. "Ignore him," he said low to Carpenter. "He wants you to give him a break during the game, he needs to remember you're not stupid."

"I heard that!" McAllister complained, and Skip looked at him and nodded like he was talking to a child.

"Yeah? 'Cause Carpenter heard you loud and clear too!"

Mac had the grace to look embarrassed. "Sorry, man," he muttered. "Skip's right, you're not stupid."

Practice evened out a bit after that, and Richie sort of moved in to take over where Mac had left off. Richie was a better teacher, giving Clay some room to do bigger things, and they were all rewarded when he blocked a few shots nobody expected him to get.

By the time they were done, Skip felt twice as worked out from running around the field to make sure everybody got their fair share of the practice, but the team was good with Carpenter, he was good with the team, and he was dripping sweat and happy at the same time.

Skip was going to call it a win.

But when Scoggins started trotting up to the parking lot for his car and waved at the team like Skip was just another guy, he didn't feel quite like he was winning much at all.

THAT NIGHT he got a text from Richie at bedtime.

Going to bed alone. Promise.

Skip smiled. He actually hadn't worried about that—not after Richie had reassured him. Richie was hot-tempered, wily, and not awesome at communication, but he wasn't a liar or a cheat.

I believe you.

How's Carpenter?

Still wheezing—but happy. You were a good teacher.

He's a good guy. Wanna pick me up tomorrow? Right after work.

Yeah, sure. Car broke?

Nope.

Skip frowned. The junkyard was out in Rancho Cordova, and Richie's parents lived in a house not far from the car yard itself. Skip didn't mind driving there—certainly not with Richie as his carrot on a stick—but since Richie had to drive down past Carmichael to get to the soccer field any—

His phone buzzed, bringing him back to the present.

Driving away sucked. Maybe it'll be easier if you drop me off.

Skip stared at his phone, mouth open.

Oh.

I doubt it. But I'll take my turn.

Thanks, Skip. See you tomorrow.

See you tomorrow.

RANCHO CORDOVA had been improved upon in the past few years. Skip remembered when he was a kid and everything past Folsom Boulevard was a Bad Place to Be. But a lot of the industrial parks had been turned into rec centers since then, and a lot of the shitty apartment complexes had been knocked down and replaced with high-end college-oriented restaurants.

But a pick-n-pull was not going to be a flower mart, no matter how much the town itself had spiffed up. The business, located out on Grant Line Boulevard, was just as remote and isolated now as it had been when Skip had first visited back in tech school.

The November sun lay thick like dust on the corpses of defunct vehicles, and Skip tried hard not to think about the ones that had gone in because of severe body damage. Had everyone survived in that one? That one? The one with the top caved in? Were the doorknobs and locks worth towing the totally demolished SUV in from wherever it had been destroyed?

The first time he'd come out here, he'd been trying to keep his mother's Oldsmobile alive, just until he got through school and could afford a car that wasn't as old as he was. Richie had helped him replace the fuel pump, the carburetor, the fuel line, the brake shoes, and pretty much every belt the damned car had. Skip liked to think he was decent with cars now, but that didn't stop his memories from filling in the blank spots of heat and cooking metal and dust and exhaust, all of which populated the pick-n-pull, even in the lengthened shadows of an autumn evening.

Richie'd texted him and said he was still at work, which meant Skip took the first left off of Grant Line after the Jacksonville split and drove in the half-mile corridor, surrounded by the blue-plastic glow of the paneling in the hurricane fencing. Eel wire topped the eight-foot fence, and Richie had once told Skip that the alarms and floodlights went off about three times a month, revealing blood on top of the eel wire and figures fleeing into the vacant fields around the junkyard at night.

When Skip got past the blue-green of the driveway, he came to the small "portable" office building where Richie worked, and oh, hey, there were the happiness chimps, standing with Richie by a new addition to the lot.

Skip parked by the small paved apron in front of the office and hustled down to where all the excitement was. Anything that involved Richie's stepbrothers, Paul and Rob, was going to be bad. In tech school Richie had needed to wear a cast for six weeks because Paul and Rob thought it was a *great* idea to ride an old chassis like a skateboard. *They'd* steered it just fine with their feet, and why couldn't Richie—who weighed a good hundred pounds less than either of the big gorillas—make that thing not hit the fucking forklift on its way down the hill?

Both guys were a good six foot five, 250 pounds of bulky muscle, and they'd been beating the shit out of Richie since he was a lean and stringy twelve-year-old.

They'd graduated, Skip thought darkly. They didn't beat him up anymore. Now they just baited him, challenged him to do stuff that was dangerous or out of his range. Richie was small, but he was strong and smart—right up until Rob or Paul said something asinine like "Hey, Richie—gotta do *this* to sit at the grown-ups table!" and Richie, who was supposed to be old enough to know better, fell for that shit like a dog fell for a ball thrown over the house. The damned dog *knew* where the ball had gone, *knew* what the other side of the house looked like, but it just kept staring up at the roofline, waiting for something to change.

The guys were both brownish—sun-streaked brown hair, skin tanned to leather, and eyes like swamp water—and Skip knew that before Richie got his tech certificate he'd burnt his fair skin again and again because maybe simply ignoring his redheaded complexion would make him tan like Paul and Rob.

Now they worked in different areas, the chimp brothers outside helping the customers find the right cars in the labyrinthine organization of car carcasses, and Richie inside the office doing the invoices or inside the garage bay maintaining the hydraulic and electronic equipment they used.

Right now *all* of them were standing in front of an old muscle car that even to Skip's untrained eye had a bent frame and metalwork that could never be repaired.

Chimp One—Paul, the oldest at twenty-eight—stood, hip cocked, an insufferable smirk on his square-jawed face as he dangled a sledgehammer from his battered paw. "I'm saying, a hood this battered, anyone can pound a hole in it—even rat-tail dogs like you, Richie!"

Richie had his arms crossed and was shaking his head at his stepbrothers like he wasn't going to do this again. "I still think you're insane, but here. Gimme the hammer and I'll try it."

Oh *fuck*.

"Richie, goddammit—" Skip started, striding across the pavement and onto the plain dirt part that held the cars. Richie cast him an oblique look and squared his jaw, and Skip started running instead.

He was too late. Richie was too short, and his strength wasn't in his torso—the sledgehammer bounced off the "sweet spot" and Richie lost control of it. His hands shot backward and he clocked himself in the face. Even Skip could hear the crunch of his broken nose.

Richie let go of the hammer, stumbled backward, and landed on his ass in the dirt, holding his bleeding nose as what Skip imagined to be a whole other ocean of pain washed over him.

Paul and Rob were laughing their asses off.

Skip crouched down by Richie and tore off his zippered work sweater. He folded it twice and gave it to Richie to hold up to his nose.

"But Skip," Richie said, his voice muffled, "it's too nice."

"Just use it," Skip directed. "If it doesn't wash, I'll buy a new one."

Richie nodded, looking confused, and Skip sighed. He saw a trip to the ER in their future, which was *not* how he'd planned to use his time tonight. But he couldn't lift Richie either. "Wait here," he muttered. "I'll drive the car down, okay?"

Richie nodded, blinking hard, and Skip stood up and turned his anger directly on the sources—who were currently laughing so hard on each other's shoulders they supported themselves by leaning against the car.

"You *assholes!*" he roared. The sledgehammer had ended up next to the car, and he grabbed it, his ire giving him some power as he hefted it easily with one hand. "He's not *weak*, he's *short*. It's not weakness, it's physics, and you two are too piss-stupid to know the difference." He hauled the sledgehammer over his shoulder and swung hard, and again, and again, pounding hole after hole after hole. Rob and Paul had stopped laughing and were backing away slowly, apparently frightened by Skip's fury as they hadn't been by Richie's bravura and pure common sense.

"Now stop acting like stupid high school bullies and start being his family, you useless pieces of gorilla shit, or *I'm* gonna show you what it's like!" With that he threw the hammer with all his might, so it shattered through the cracked windscreen of the car with a crash and bounced harmlessly off the corroded floorboards.

He was breathing hard, and he could feel a faint ping in his shoulder that might hurt in the morning, but mostly he was glad he wasn't holding the sledgehammer anymore so he couldn't hurl it through their stupid fucking heads.

"Skip?"

Skip turned, dreamlike, and saw that Richie had pushed himself up and wobbled next to him. "You'rb pweddy hard-gore, you-nno?"

Skip sighed, some of his mad leaving, and he threw a gentle arm over Richie's shoulder. "Yeah? Well, be sure to tell the soccer team. C'mon. Where's your duffel?"

"'S'inside," Richie mumbled. "Gaw... *no'* wha' I wanna do!"

"Yeah, well, remember that next time," Skip maneuvered him to the passenger seat of his car.

Richie's dad and stepmom were inside the office, smoking and counting the till. Skip was just going to jog inside and grab Richie's stuff without a word, but Richie's dad, Ike, made the mistake of talking to him.

"Wait—who *are* you?"

"I'm Richie's friend—I've been here before," Skip said briefly, although he'd probably been by the house more often to pick Richie up and go somewhere. Okay—there, behind the desk. He'd spotted it. He brushed by Ike and Kay Scoggins and tried not to choke on the clouds of smoke that rolled off both of them. "He was gonna crash at my place tonight since we've got soccer in the morning."

Ike decided he was going to put his squat fireplug of a body between Skip and that goddamned duffel bag, and Skip realized how much of his anger *hadn't* cleared when he'd pitched the sledgehammer through the window.

"Well why can't Richie get his own goddamned duffel bag?" Ike demanded. "He's got to send his pansy-assed friend to get his shit for him?"

"Richie is *bleeding* in the front of my car because *her* useless fucktarded kids dared him into the emergency room again. It's a little too late for you to pretend to watch out for your son, isn't it? You want to actually give a shit about your kid, how about pay him more than minimum going rate for his job and not make him feel like shit for something he can't do anything about! Jesus!" Because Skip had heard them both razzing on Richie's height, his red hair, his pug nose—all the things that Skip had just discovered he really really treasured, he'd heard Richie's father put down.

"Wait," Kay said, stepping out from behind the desk. She was a whip-thin woman with shoe-black hair who wore bright nylon-

and-foam push-up bras under her loose V-necked T-shirts. She liked to lean forward at the desk and squish her cleavage forward because she probably thought that heightened her allure. "What about my kids?"

"Tell them to stay off his back," Skip snapped, and he must have had some extra force in his voice or something, because he was able to reach past Ike and snag Richie's bag. "I'll drop him off at work Monday morning. I don't trust any of you people to take care of him before then."

And with that he left, not caring if they remembered him— although he'd been there more than once and had done his best to be civil during those times. Hell, Ike Scoggins had even picked Richie up at Skip's house once, when Richie had helped Skip move in, but so what?

All he cared about *now* was that Richie was in the front of his car bleeding, and Skip had three nights and two days to make sure he was okay.

RICHIE HAD Kaiser, just like Skip, and they lucked out. There were no drive-by shootings, multicar pileups, or plague viruses that night, so they got out of there by ten o'clock with a CT scan and a check for a concussion under their belts. Richie's nose was bandaged with a brace and everything. Skipper had hold of his pain meds and some strict instructions *not* to let him do anything too strenuous like, say, play soccer like a screaming banshee or ride someone's shoulders up and down the field if his team won.

Skip stopped at an In-N-Out for burgers on the way home, making sure to get Richie the large chocolate shake and animal-style fries. He got himself a double ham, no cheese, no sauce, with a Diet Coke.

Richie sighed as Skip handed him the bag. "You're not even going to pig out and help me with my fries?" Some of the swelling had gone down since the doc had set his nose, and his voice was muffled but not distorted.

"I might when we get home," Skip said, admitting that the smell coming off the bag was heavenly. "Right now, I just want to get home and feed Hazel and...."

"And what?" Richie asked, his voice small.

"And hold you, Richie. Damn—I saw that sledgehammer bounce and thought it was going to smash your face completely. You'd be breathing out of a tube right now!" Skip's hands tightened on the steering wheel, and he shivered. He'd given Richie his sweatshirt to bleed on, and he'd been freezing all night.

"You want to hold me?" Richie asked, his voice brightening even under the swelling and the bandages. "Because seriously, that's all I've wanted all day."

Skip consciously relaxed his hands and moved his right one to Richie's knee. "Me too," he said. "I mean, I wanted the... you know...." His face heated. "But more than that...."

Richie covered Skip's hand with his own. "Yeah. Yeah. Me too."

The only thing either one of them said after that was "Turn up the heater, Skip. You're making me shiver just looking at you."

That was nice, having Richie look after him too.

THEY ATE quietly in Skip's awful kitchen. Then Skip cleaned up and urged Richie to bed. "I'm going to shower first," he said. The doctor had told Richie to stay out of the hot water until the next morning.

"Ugh," Richie groaned. "How can you even stand me! I must smell like an armpit—I'll sleep on the couch!"

"Don't you dare," Skip said quickly. "Look, I'll skip the shower tonight, okay? Just...."

Richie was looking at him through the mask of gauze and bruising under his eyes.

"Just be where I can touch you," Skip finished, feeling stupid.

They climbed into bed together still wearing their boxers, and Skip spooned Richie while they watched the shows that had been recorded while they'd been at Kaiser.

"You ever notice how these guys get shot and keep running after the bad guys?" Richie mumbled in disgust.

"*So* not how it works," Skip said with feeling. He tightened his arm around Richie's middle, feeling the pinged muscle he'd strained when he'd been wielding the sledgehammer.

"Yeah, but I always think it *is*, right before I do something stupid."

Skip chuckled, and Richie reached for the phone he'd put on the bed stand. "It's my dad," he said, looking at the text. "He wants me to come home."

Skip growled.

"I'm staying at Skip's this weekend, as planned," Richie read as he texted. "Doc said I needed rest."

"Yeah, well, I thought you needed something else," Skip jibed. "Seriously, way to kill a mood."

Richie patted the hand Skip had clasped around his middle. "Yeah, yeah. I can still give you a victory hand job, don't get your panties in a knot."

Skip chuffed air into the back of Richie's neck, and Richie laughed softly. Then his phone buzzed.

"Skip, what did you say to my dad?"

Skip grunted. "I may or may not have called your stepbrothers fucktarded pieces of useless gorilla shit," he confessed. "And I might have said something about them not being assholes to you—after that it's all getting fuzzy."

Richie risked a look behind him. "Ouch! Well I'll just tell him you're sorry—"

"Don't press Send on that!" Skip protested. "I'm not even a little bit sorry!"

"But you can't just leave things like that—this is my family!"

"Family treats you better," Skip muttered. *If I was family, I'd treat you so much better than that, Richie.*

"How would you kn—" Richie stopped and sighed, but Skipper heard the rest anyway.

Stung, he rolled over and tried to concentrate on the car commercial on television. Behind him, he heard Richie texting viciously, and then Richie shoved up so he was sitting and started to talk into the phone like he was in the middle of a conversation.

"Yeah, I know what he said—he was mad, and he was worried about me. He's my friend, what? He doesn't get to be worried about me? Yeah, I know it was stupid to—wait."

Richie's frantic tap on Skip's arm got Skip to roll over.

"I didn't throw the sledgehammer through the car," Richie said, squinting through all the bandages in confusion. "The guys dared me to hit the hood, and that's all I remember."

At Skip's grimace, Richie's eyes widened. "I don't remember that!" he mouthed. Well, he probably didn't—he'd been pretty spacey until after they left Kaiser.

"I was pissed," Skip muttered. "They were laughing at you."

"Yeah," Richie said into the phone. "The guys were laughing after I got hurt. It flipped a switch in Skipper. He gets protective like that. I'm not making him apologize for shit. I'll see you Monday, Dad. Maybe you cool off a minute and remember who really *did* get hurt."

Richie hit End Call with a grunt of disgust. "The guy who showed up to get me because I was a goddamned pussy who didn't like saying good-bye. *That's* who got hurt." He reached out and stroked Skipper's cheek. "Sorry I was an asshole about your family," he said, his voice soft.

Skipper shook his head like it was no big deal. "You're the one with your nose in a sling," he said, trying to be funny. "Do you need a pain med or—"

"Stop trying to mother me, Christopher," Richie said gravely, and even the fact that "pher" sounded like "brur" through his broken nose didn't change that almost magical impact of hearing his real name. Skip stopped moving and Richie pushed his hair back from his forehead. "You take real good care of me. I just… I need to remember you don't have anyone to take care of you. You… you need someone."

Skipper smiled a little, a real try this time. "I… you know. If you ever want the job."

Richie nodded. "Yeah, well, I get the feeling this here is part of the audition." He ran his fingers through Skip's yellow hair again, like he enjoyed that. "I'll try not to fuck it up too much from here on in. Now spoon me again, the show's almost on."

Skip did as ordered, appreciating all over again the joys of Richie's hard, stringy body mashed up against his own.

He must have been tired then—they both must have been tired—because before the fourth act, before the bad guy was revealed and captured, the two of them closed their eyes in the darkened room and fell asleep.

Stormy Night

IT WAS a good thing Carpenter had just been inducted—he ended up playing the entire game as a defender, and Owens moved into Richie's spot as forward. They got destroyed—of course they got destroyed—but since even McAllister let a few through and Singh could only catch so many attempts, there was nothing they could do about that.

After the game, during the obligatory pizza and beer, Richie told Carpenter that Skip had to bail on his date so he could take care of him. Then he told the whole damned world about Skip throwing a sledgehammer through a car windshield, even though he still didn't remember what actually happened.

"Skipper?" Galvan said, raising an elegant black eyebrow in a handsomely chiseled Latino face. "*Skipper* threw a sledgehammer through a windshield. Are you sure this wasn't a hallucination?" Galvan's eyes twinkled as he manipulated the top of Richie's head and pretended to be checking both eyes. "People imagine all sorts of things with a concussion!"

Richie shook his head (not too hard—he'd admitted privately to Skip that he had a motherfucker of a headache and not even the pain meds could completely squash it) and waved his hands. "Swear, it wasn't me who said it—it was my *dad*. Apparently Skipper saw the chimp brothers cracking up while I was bleeding in the dust and lost his fucking mind."

Skip felt his face heat. "They were being assholes," he mumbled. That got him a whole lot of laughter, some claps on the back, and offers to buy more beer.

"Good to know you got our backs off the field, Skip," Owens said, toasting them with a microbrew.

Skip refrained from saying that Richie was sort of a special case, and Jimenez spoke up about how to avoid property damage because you could get sued for that. Well, Jimenez *was* a lawyer. Thomas, their schoolteacher with a scruffy brown beard and a man-bun, started asking him questions about that. Apparently Thomas had some students in trouble.

As the rest of the team broke into smaller groups of involved conversation, Richie confessed—not privately this time—that his head hurt. The offered beers were given a rain check and Skip and Richie went home instead. They'd played in the morning mist, but as Skip drove home in the early evening, rain was already setting in.

"Sorry about your head," he apologized, squinting as the drops hit the windshield.

"My head doesn't feel that bad," Richie said impishly. "I just wanted you to myself."

Skip grimaced, still concentrating on the road. "Sorry about that victory hand job—maybe we can do that next week."

From the corner of his eye, he saw Richie smirk. "Yeah, well, I understand that pity hand jobs are even more awesome. Wanna see?"

Skipper found himself smiling. "Can we wait until we get home?" he asked, pretty sure this was a yes since they both wanted to live.

"Yes, but barely," Richie said, voice sober.

They managed to get inside, dashing through the rain, before Skipper tried a gentle, sore-nose-friendly kiss.

Richie returned it just as gently, and Skip pulled away and smiled, feeling on even keel for the first time since he'd seen Richie with the sledgehammer. Carefully, he framed Richie's face with his palms. "I've been waiting for that," he said softly.

"Just the kiss?" Richie hopefully palmed Skipper through his sweats.

"Well, that too," Skipper said, his brains somewhat scrambled by the kiss and Richie's firm touch. "You want I should shower?"

Richie shook his head. "Naw," he whispered and kissed Skip again, pushing him back to the couch. Skip sat down abruptly when the backs of his knees hit, and Richie's busy hands were lifting Skip's sweatshirt and T-shirt up and over his head. He shivered for a moment—the heater hadn't kicked in and the clouded light from outside was not enough to warm the darkened room. Then Richie licked gently, delicately, at Skip's chest and his teeth closed around Skip's nipple, although he didn't suckle. Skip let out a needy sound he wasn't proud of.

Oh! He hadn't imagined this, had he? Richie's touch—a lot more confident now than last week—so rough, so exquisite, that Skip moaned. He pulled in a breath and tried to control himself, but he'd waited, wanting, studying every text like ancient Sanskrit, trying not to weenie out like a teenager over their exchanges.

He clasped Richie's head to his chest and arched his hips.

"Shh...." Richie moved up, and Skip, mindful of his injuries, let go immediately.

"It's okay," Richie whispered against his ear. "I'm here."

He tilted Skip's jaw and moved in to kiss some more, and in the meantime slid his hand down Skip's pants. His hand was rough and cold, his grip no-bullshit.

"Ah...." Skip breathed. "Ah.... God, Richie. Gonna shoot like *now*!"

Richie chuckled and licked his neck. "You said you didn't get hard. I remember. You don't have that problem with me, do you?"

"Not even," Skip breathed.

Richie shifted his weight on the couch and his grip on Skip's cock went away. Skip opened his eyes and Richie had shoved his own jeans down to his feet and was kicking them off with his shoes. His cock was mostly full, and Skip didn't need Richie's hand, urgent, driving him to touch it.

It was the thing that had been missing from his grip all week.

He stroked slowly, strongly, and Richie's shaky "nungh" in his ear intoxicated like alcohol, but it sent him higher. Richie's grip resumed, and then Richie, always enterprising, swung a leg over his hips so they were cock to cock.

"Your hands are bigger," Richie rasped. It was maybe the only time he'd heard Richie confess that there was something he couldn't do.

Skip wrapped his hand around the two of them, feeling Richie's length against his. Oh God, there was something erotic, raw, and carnal about their *cocks* grinding together.

"You feel so good," Skip whispered. "Ah, God, Richie, this is...."

Richie grunted and thrust inside the circle of Skip's fingers, his movements slow and intense. With a little cry, he broke, thrusting in a quick frenzy, but Skip knew it wasn't going to do it. This thing, this was *amazing*—but it wasn't going to bring them to orgasm.

Skip let go of their members, then leaned up and pulled Richie down on him. "Shh," he whispered. "Do you have lube in your pocket?"

Richie looked up and smiled, his eyes crinkling above the mask. Then his expression fell. "I'm not supposed to... you know... get too... jiggled."

Skip smiled, nuzzling his cheek. "Just sit on me and move slow," he whispered. "I'll stroke you."

Richie flashed that mask-broken smile again and rifled through his jeans on the ground. He came up with a little pocket bottle of lubricant, which he offered to Skip. He straddled Skip's middle again, turning so he was facing away.

"You wanna, uh...." He rested his cheek gently against Skip's knee and started to stroke Skip's cock—not too fast. Skip knew he was trying not to make the ride too rough, and Richie *definitely* didn't want Skip's thing in his mouth, not now when his whole face was pretty tender.

But Skip got to run his hands down Richie's ribs, over his thighs, and around his backside, which was replete in ginger fur.

Richie hugged Skipper's knee tight like he was trying to hide. "I'm sort of a furry little bastard," he apologized, as though maybe Skip hadn't noticed the past few times they'd been naked.

"I like all of you," Skip said throatily. He lubed up his fingers and teased Richie's pucker.

Richie let out a little "Ah... ah... ah...."

"That part too," Skip whispered.

"Definitely!"

"You like that part?"

"Definitely means 'more now,'" Richie cracked gruffly. "Ah... oh man... that's... that's good...."

Skip stretched him gently, waiting until the rim around his fingers was slack and open. Richie continued his maddeningly uneven stroke on Skip's cock. Skip had to keep himself from arching into that caress, turning it into the whole meal when it was supposed to be a snack.

"You ready?" He moved his fingers and slid both thumbs inside. Richie's muscles clamped down on him and Richie groaned, turning his head and biting the inside of Skip's knee.

"God.... Skip... oh Jesus...."

Skip pulled out quickly and wiped his fingers on the inside of the sweats sitting next to him on the couch. Richie moaned and his arms shook as he braced himself on Skip's knee and swung his leg over. The face he turned toward Skipper glistened with sweat.

Skip gripped Richie's thighs as Richie positioned himself with his knees on either side of Skip's hips. He rose slightly and placed Skip's cock right there, at his warm, loosened entrance. Part of the head slid in and then stopped, and Richie leaned his head back, mouth parted, eyes closed, and hissed softly as he slid down.

Halfway. He grunted and raised himself, the friction driving Skipper a little crazy. He had to force his hips to stay planted as Richie lowered himself again, a little lower.

And up.

And a little lower.

And up.

And.... "Ahh." Skipper groaned, long and low, as Richie slid all the way down this time. He stopped, quivering, impaled on Skipper's erection. His cock, red and fully erect, splatted lightly on Skip's lower abdomen in time with Richie's breathing.

"Damn, Richie," Skip said, part in admiration and part in agony. "That's... you're so good...."

"I want to move," Richie moaned. "But... I can't...." He shifted his hips back and forth, Skipper rubbing inside him but not stroking, not the way they both wanted. Oh. Of course. He couldn't rock himself that hard—not with every bounce jarring his sore head.

"Rise up," Skip muttered. "About halfway. Prop yourself up on the couch and sit still."

Richie complied, both of them breathing delicately as he moved. Then Richie grabbed the back of the couch with one hand and planted his other hand on Skip's shoulder. Skip grabbed his slim hips, held firmly, and then started to thrust.

Slow, slow, slow, hard, slow, slow, slow, hard....

Not too hard. Not too fast. Slow, slow, slow, hard.

Richie started to whisper and beg, but Skipper couldn't go any faster. No knocking about his head—that was the golden rule.

"C'mon... faster... c'mon, Skip, faster... harder... oh please... please... please.... Skipper...."

He was begging—*begging*, his voice cracking—and Skip couldn't stand it anymore. "Grab yourself, Richie. As fast as you can. Fuck your own fist, dammit, jack yourself off—"

"*Yes*...."

Skip continued—slow, slow, slow, *hard*, slow, slow, slow, *hard*—as his body screamed with the need to go faster, harder, to come, dammit, *come*! And Richie's hand flew on his own cock as he gibbered, "Fuck fuck fuck fuck.... *Skipper*!"

Slow, slow, *hard, hard, hard, hard, hard*....

"Oh my God, *yes*!"

Skipper had to close his eyes because Richie's come splashed up—it hit Skip's chest, his mouth, his cheeks, and his hair. It missed Skip's eyes, but Skip kept them closed anyway. Richie's ass clenched and convulsed around Skipper's cock, and that was Skipper's edge.

Skipper moaned, his entire body suffusing with light as a long, slow, shattering orgasm rolled through him and spurted out of his cock, into Richie.

"Oh God," he breathed, and Richie leaned carefully into him, not jouncing. Skipper raised his hands to cup Richie's upper arms, moving his palms in small circles.

"How's your head?" he asked, concerned. Hand jobs. This was supposed to be a pity hand job.

"Hurts," Richie muttered. "I'll take some pain meds. In a thousand years."

Skipper laughed and pushed Richie's hair back from his face. He nuzzled Richie's cheek, smelling their sex—and ass sex had a smell, there was no mistaking—and Richie's definitive redhead sweat.

And over all of it, permeating their pores, the smell of wood smoke and rain, as night fell and the world stormed around them.

"Richie?"

"Yeah?"

He blinked hard against the darkness and the spots still flying about his vision. "That was magic. Don't laugh."

Oh God. He should have said "Don't laugh" first.

But Richie cupped his cheeks and held him for a sloppy, come-tinted kiss. He came up for air and smiled faintly. "Not laughing," he whispered. "Magic. It's real. I never knew."

He rested his head on Skipper's shoulder for a moment then, and together they listened to the rain.

THEY TOOK showers after that, and Skip had just finished heating some soup and baking a cornbread mix when the power went out. They ate a quiet dinner in the dark and then slid into bed, their shorts still on, and began to talk.

It was funny—they'd known each other for six years. You would have thought they knew everything, right? But Richie's weight, warm and comforting against Skip's shoulder, seemed to free him to ask questions men didn't usually ask. And the darkness—or maybe the comfort of Skip's arm around his shoulders—seemed to do the same for Richie.

"So," Richie said, voice comfortable and drowsy, "I don't get it. Why'd your dad leave you with your mom if she was a mess?"

Skip grunted. "Well, he was probably the reason she was a mess. He… I mean he provided, and he wasn't mean, but I remember—he'd play with me and watch television and basically be a dad with me after work, but he wouldn't...." This had never been so clear to Skipper as it was now, when he couldn't hardly stand to see Richie on the field when they couldn't at least brush their hands together. "They never touched," he said at last, his voice aching in the darkness. "All I want to do when I see you is touch you—any part of you—even if it's just bumping your shoulder. But they—they never touched. And I think she got lonely, after so many years of that. They needed to touch."

Richie hummed a little and turned on his side. Skipper matched him so they were looking at each other in the dark, the patter of rain loud against the black windows.

"My mom used to whore around," he said, quiet, like a kid afraid of being caught telling a dirty word. "I mean, my dad used to accuse her of it, and there were guys all the time. Wasn't supposed to tell nobody about Uncle Billy or Bobby or what-the-fuck-ever. Anyway, she finally took off with that last one, and dad hooked up with Kay and...." Richie's mouth compressed.

"She whores around on him?"

He blew out a breath. "I wish. Mostly she's just… just not warm, you know?"

Skip remembered that whip-thin person who didn't seem to be concerned at all that Richie was bleeding. "Yeah, I know," he said grimly.

"Was your mom warm?"

Skip swallowed against the lump suddenly in his throat. "Yeah," he whispered. "She… I mean, even at the end, when she was coughing up blood and just wouldn't quit drinking… she'd call me into her room at the end of the day and she'd be lying down, a cloth on her head. She'd say, 'Tell me what you did today,' and I'd...." This was embarrassing. "I made up stuff, mostly," he said, grimacing. "She didn't know the difference. I was this fat kid with zits from like, seventh grade on. Nobody gave a shit if I was there, really, until my complexion cleared and my growth spurt hit, about my junior year. But I told her I was on the track team or the football team, and all the time I would have been practicing, I was working at that burger shack—you know the one on Madison? It's all boarded up now, but they hired me and fudged the whole work permit thing. Part of the reason I was so fat, really, because it's all I ate for about three years, but it was food."

"But she wanted to know?" Richie asked, like he was making sure.

Skip nodded. "Yeah. She did. You?"

"My dad," Richie said, voice rough. "I mean, he wasn't always nice about it, but he'd ask about grades, and he'd always give me quarters to go play video games at the pizza parlor if I got good ones." He rolled his eyes. "Paul and Rob used to steal them, but still. He was trying. It was like, the whole reason he married Kay was because he thought we could be a family, like we couldn't be with my real mom. Wasn't his fault. Just the wrong damned person. For me, anyway."

"So you had someone too," Skip said, feeling good about that. "Good."

Richie was quiet for a moment, his eyes searching Skip's in the darkness. "Yeah, that's great that we had someone when we were kids, Christopher, but I don't think either one of us had somebody to tell us what to do about this—what we're doing right here."

"Lying in the dark telling secrets?" Skip asked, trailing his fingertips over Richie's cheek.

Richie grabbed his hand. "Having sex because we can't stand not to touch," he said, voice raw, and Skip pulled their hands to his mouth, where he placed a chaste kiss on the end of Richie's fingertips.

"I think we're falling in—"

Richie pressed his fingers against Skip's lips. "Don't," he ordered hoarsely. "You say it and it'll have a name. I'm not ready for it to have a name yet, Skip. I've got to tell my father a name, and I'm not ready for that."

Skip swallowed, that lump in his throat that had formed when he'd talked about his mom growing tighter. His eyes burned, and he made to roll away. Richie stilled him with a warm hand on his bicep. Skip turned to him and searched his face, wondering if his own eyes were as bright in the dark as Richie's.

"Here," Richie whispered, tilting his head. "In my ear. No one can hear it but me."

Skip had never said these words to a girl. He'd never lain awake at night with a girl in his bed, talking about his awful childhood or the best parts that had sat like diamonds in mud, bright and shiny, to pull him through.

But the hollow of Richie's ear was a secret cave, and the words came so easy in the absolute shelter of the unlit night.

"I'm falling in love with you, Richie," he whispered, steeling himself for not hearing the words back.

"Me too, Skip," Richie said, his lips brushing Skip's ear. "I promise not to tell."

"Me too."

They lay there for a long time before they fell asleep, looking at each other's faces in the shadows, breathing in the silence, listening to the rain fall.

Sorta Thankful

THEY STAYED inside the next day, hung out, watched television, and made slow, sweet love—Skip could call it that in his head, because he'd said the words. Maybe it was the slowness, because of Richie's head, or maybe it was the melancholy of the rain, but somehow every touch became magnified, a mix of pleasure and pain.

They still laughed and still cracked jokes, but early, *early* Monday morning, right before they left for Skip to drop Richie off, Richie slid in front of the door really quick and blocked it.

He stood there, looking up at Skipper, bandage and nose brace still on and the black bruises underneath his eyes still swollen.

His full mouth—split lip and all—was curved faintly up, though, and his bright eyes were unusually sober. "You gotta kiss me now," he said. "Make it your best one, because it's gotta last until Friday since we don't kiss on Thursdays, okay?"

Skip nodded and refrained from whining about how they'd started out by kissing on Thursday. They'd been lucky—so lucky—not to get caught. For a moment a frisson of fear passed through him as he wondered what would happen to soccer—not just winter ball but his entire team of people that he'd forged through six years of just not giving up—if someone saw him and Richie kissing.

I'd give them up for Richie, he thought. *But if I lose him, they're all I've got.*

Just that suddenly, he realized what a precarious place they were in.

But Richie was still gazing up at him like he could make this kiss—this one kiss at the end of a weekend of playing like they were a family—last. *Skipper* could do that. He was the one with the magic, apparently, because he could make the next five days not ache without kisses.

He tried.

He cupped Richie's neck gently and tilted his jaw up with firm thumbs, and then tasted. Richie'd eaten the same breakfast he had, so toast and eggs went away. That left Richie with the faint antiseptic of the bandages in his smell, but he was still warm and vibrant, tangy, alive. Skip tasted it slow and deep, just like fucking this weekend, but softer. He wasn't trying to hit any spots, there was no fantastic come in the center of the goal box, there was just Richie and the animal noises he was making and the way his fingers scrabbled on Skip's shoulders like he was clinging for dear life.

With a cry, Richie broke it off, his eyes wide and shocked and running over.

"That was a horrible thing to do to me," he said, voice broken. "Kissing me like that. How am I going to live without that for another day? Or two? Much less five. Dammit, Skipper, you're gonna fucking break me." He turned and grabbed his duffel bag and dashed out into the rain.

Skipper barely managed to keep Hazel from escaping before he followed, but he was so wrecked he forgot his jacket and his lunch. The drive to Rancho was one long, miserable, cold and wet trip, timed by the thump of the wiper blades and harshened by Richie's recriminating silence.

"I'm sorry," he said after they'd gone over Highway 50. "I... I wanted to give you a kiss to last."

"It wasn't your fault," Richie said, his voice still thick. "I... I should have known... you can't make kisses last, not like that. Maybe if you were going off to war or something and I knew I *had* to be without you. But you're just down the fucking road, and I'm trying to remember why it makes any sense."

Skipper had to be the one who said it. "You were right, you know. I'm the one who doesn't have any family but the team. You're the one with family. *And* you've got the team to lose. You've got to...."

"What?" Richie asked, sounding bitter. "What is it I've got to do?"

Now Skipper felt near tears too. "Nothing, Richie. Just... you know. See me when you can."

84

They were driving out near Grant Line now, and Richie's hand on his knee surprised him.

"I'll do that," he said throatily.

Skip risked a glance at Richie's face. In a shift of mood like mercury, he'd suddenly brightened.

"What are you thinking?" Skip asked, peering ahead for the pick-n-pull.

"I'm thinking that I've got someone who wants to see me this weekend. I'm not gonna fuck it up by being a big old emo bitch."

Skip smiled a little. "Just because we're gay doesn't mean you're bitchy," he said, and Richie's gasp hit him like a slap.

"What?" he asked, but it was time to turn and he couldn't look at Richie because he was too busy watching for that stupid fucking car that didn't turn on its lights in the rain.

And there, the car had passed and he could gun it onto the big mudslide that the junkyard had become. Skip hoped people had fun rooting through the dead cars in the rain, because he couldn't think of anything he'd less like to do, unless it was root through them when it was 120 in the shade.

Skip was halfway up the track before he risked a look at Richie again. Richie was staring straight ahead, mouth slightly parted, face pale against his spectacular hair.

"What—Richie, are you okay? You're not going to throw up, are you?"

Richie shook himself and then looked at Skipper with a sort of green smile. Skip had to pull his attention back to the road, which was more slippery than the eel wire above them, and when he finally pulled to a stop at the five-car parking lot, he looked at Richie again.

"Richie, do I need to take you to the doctor? Should I tell your dad you're gonna hurl? What in the—"

Richie stopped him with a surprise kiss—hurried, and very mindful that they could get caught, but definitely a kiss on the corner of his mouth. Skip turned his head, stunned, and Richie thrust his tongue in once and tasted, and then withdrew, running a thumb over Skip's lips before reaching behind them to the backseat for his duffel.

85

"Uh...."

Richie gave a slightly more natural smile. "You're right, Skip. We're gay. We said queer before, and I don't know why saying gay is different, but it is to me. Nobody put *that* name on it before. See you Thursday."

With that he was gone, trotting across the parking lot to the offices, which he opened with a key. Skip waited until he turned and waved at the doorway and then disappeared before heading out.

On his way, about halfway through the blue-green corridor of plastic and eel wire, he moved to the side and let a tow truck by, Richie's dad at the helm. It was then that he realized the big chance Richie had taken with that kiss and all, and he felt slightly better as he got back to Grant Line and drove away.

They were gay. That had a name—and Skip didn't know why, but if the word *gay* made it clearer to Richie, it made it clearer to Skip. Sometimes it was like hearing a person's first name as opposed to his last name or his nickname. Scoggins was the guy Skip screamed at on the soccer field—but *Richie* was the guy who came apart in Skip's arms. A kid named Christopher was a dime a dozen—but a kid named *Skip*, that kid could do something, right? So maybe to Richie, *queer* meant one thing and *gay* meant another; Skip didn't care. If it helped make Richie okay inside, Skip would take any name Richie needed to hear.

Anyway, it wasn't so bad having a name—you could deal with shit when you had a name. They could look up "gay" on the Internet and see what positions they could try (although Skip was pretty sure they'd figure most of those out on their own) or they could read books about people coming out and see what that was like.

They could watch movies or television and follow politics—although watching a movie about being gay did not really appeal to Skip, and neither did following politics. But it was a thing they could *do* if they needed to see how the rest of the world handled being what they *were*.

At any rate, they were not just "Skip and Richie versus the entire straight world," they were "Skip and Richie, gay guys who might or might not have an entire community they could join."

He wondered somewhat mournfully if there was a gay rec soccer league they could join if his guys decided they weren't progressive enough to deal with "Skip and Richie, gay guys who thought they already had a community and were now somewhat adrift."

The entire exchange left him fretful and out of sorts, though. He'd forgotten his jacket and his lunch, which meant he had to run through the rain from his car to the building, and then again at lunch to the healthy sandwich place. He went with Carpenter during lunch, and Carpenter was willing to lend him his umbrella, but Skip declined because Carpenter hadn't even brought a hat. By the time they got back, Skipper was shaking a little and sneezing a lot and still staring at his phone during every break he got.

"Tesko Tech," he said for the umpteenth time, as his head grew bigger and more swollen and the world around him turned into an icebox. "This is Skipper Keith, how can I help you?"

"Oh Schipperke!" said that now familiar voice. "You're not sounding good, young man. What are you even doing at work?"

"I'll pick up some cold meds on my way home," Skip defended, but he knew what it sounded like was "Ob by bay hobe." Oh hells. This was gonna be a doozy. "Can I help you?" *Cab I helb boo?* Oh Jesus, with any luck, Skipper's cold would make this guy think twice about hitting on him, right?

"You can let me bring you some hot tea and chicken soup," Mr. Flirtation said, sounding serious. "You don't sound good at all! Seriously—you guys are downstairs in the west wing of the building, right? Let me have someone run that to you. Please tell me you've got somebody to take care of you when you get home."

Skipper groaned and rested his aching head in his arms. "Who *abbre* boo?" he asked, completely unable to think of what he was supposed to be saying. "Whe abre boo so nife too bee?"

"Why am I so nice to you?" the caller laughed. "Because you've got a friendly voice, Skip. And because you actually talked me through my problem even after I hit on you shamelessly. You're a really good sport, by the way. Now seriously, give my secretary ten minutes, she'll be down with some Theraflu Daytime. But *please* tell me your girlfriend is going to be home to hold your hand, because you're the first friend I've made here at Tesko, and I'm sort of hoping you're taken care of."

Oh, that was sweet. Wasn't that sweet? Skip should text Richie and tell him that his horrible flirty gay-porn-watching ass-groper was really a sweetheart who just liked to tease.

"By boyfwend cabn't comb till Fwiday," he said mournfully. "Bub ith nife ob boo too athk."

"Aw, Schipperke," his caller said gently, "that sucks. I hope the Theraflu works. Make sure you take tomorrow off, okay? As bad as you sound, you're going to need to rest."

"Thabk boo," Skip said, not wanting to raise his head off his desk. "Thabs nithe. Hab a nithe bay!"

He hung up and groaned, and his phone beeped at the same time he looked up and saw Carpenter standing over his desk with a company sweatshirt, Skip's size.

"Hey," he said weakly. "Ith tha' for be?"

"Yeah," Carpenter said, looking unusually sober. "Here, Skip— let's get it on. You look like death. You should have made Richie wait while you put on a jacket."

Skip blinked and tried to remember what they'd told Carpenter about Richie coming over to his house. He couldn't focus that far.

"Ricthie wad pithed," he said, and then he looked at the phone. *Sorry I was a bitch this morning.*

Skip smiled and some of his misery fell away.

"Bud not abymore," he said, huddling into the new sweatshirt. *Not a bitch*, he texted. *Still love you.*

Me too.

He stroked the phone for a moment, smiling and losing track of what Carpenter was doing until he heard a cleared throat. At that moment, a very efficient-looking woman in her fifties strode up on no-nonsense pumps.

"Mr. Keith?" she asked, her crisp voice tempered with kindness. "Yeb?"

She smiled a little, and for a moment her lean face with the tastefully bleached hair wavered and she was his mother, older than her years and blurring like a watercolor in the dimness of her bedroom.

"Hi. My boss sent me here with some Theraflu for you. He's worried you won't make it home either." She handed him a big steaming mug with the company logo on the outside and hopefully a whole lot of super drugged-up goodness on the inside.

"I can take him home," Carpenter said easily. "I'll call his boyfriend too."

Skip paused right before he sipped and looked at Carpenter in surprise, but the nice woman who really didn't look like his mother at all was striding off already, and Carpenter was looking at him with gentle understanding.

Skip sipped his Theraflu for a few moments, not able to answer that soft, insistent stare.

"This is really working," he said after a little while. "I can probably finish out my shift and get myself home." Oh God. He could *breathe* again.

"So I shouldn't call Richie?" Carpenter said levelly, and Skip risked a glance up.

Carpenter was just… waiting. Not judgy or anything, just waiting.

"I'll text him when I get home," Skip said, trying to laugh it off. His head still hurt, and his stomach, and his hands felt shaky as hell. He was still sick—the medicine hadn't changed that, it had just made it easier to function.

He was going to have to get him some of that, and he was already planning what to buy.

Right as soon as Carpenter stopped waiting.

"You could have told me," Carpenter said at last, sighing and making to go back to his own cubicle, where an entire row of lights was blinking for him.

"It just happened," Skip said, surprising himself. "Right before Halloween. It's… you know." He laughed humorlessly. "My gentleman caller knows. Richie and me…."

Carpenter grimaced and looked back at him. "You and Richie are still figuring shit out," he said astutely.

Skip's face heated even beyond the fever. "You're very smart," he said.

Carpenter nodded and smiled, some of the tension easing from the air. "And you're the only person who's ever treated me like that," he said. "If you ever need a friend—"

"I know where you work." Skipper managed a smile and a wink.

Carpenter gave him a thumbs-up and picked up his phone, and barely, Skip made it through work.

He stopped and picked up some Theraflu on the way home, and some NyQuil, and some green tea and some cider vinegar and some plain old Advil. His head was already aching as he walked through the door, and he groaned. He'd been planning on going running that night, since Richie sort of threw his workout regimen into disarray, and he hated calling in sick. He figured he'd hunker down, drug himself, go to bed, and hopefully wake up the next day feeling better.

He lay under the covers shivering for a while, hoping the medicine would take effect eventually, petting Hazel until drool caught in her smoky black cat beard and texting Richie. Every now and then he fell asleep between texts, and when he woke up Richie would be asking him why he wasn't keeping up with their show.

Sorry. Falling asleep.

It's only eight o'clock!

*Too much good exercise this weekend. *leer**

Fine.

Did I tell you that guy called today? He thought I was sick and was actually really nice. Sent his secretary down with tea and everything.

His phone rang.

"He sent his secretary down with tea?" Richie asked sharply.

"Yeah," Skip said, hoping his meds had kicked in and he didn't sound pathetic. "It was nice. Carpenter got me a company jacket. Don't worry. I was just going to go to sleep early and I'll be fine in the morning."

"He didn't try to hit on you again?" Richie said, sounding grumpy.

"Mostly he just said I was a nice guy who put up with him and then asked if my girlfriend was taking care of me."

"What did you say?" Richie asked, sounding upset and curious at the same time.

God, Skip's head hurt. He had no subterfuge in him. "I said my boyfriend couldn't take care of me until Friday, so don't worry."

"'Til *Friday!*"

"Richie, don't sweat it!" Skip said sharply. "Look, man. My head hurts, and some sort of night thing I took is making me loopy. I'm going to bed before I start seeing little green men, okay?"

"You call me in the morning and let me know how you are, okay?"

Skip smiled. This beat the hell out of the last time he was sick, before Carpenter started working at Tesko even. Skip was pretty sure back then he could have died in his bed and nobody would have noticed until soccer practice Thursday.

"I promise," he slurred.

He fell asleep with the light on, curled around the phone. When he woke up at four in the morning, it was because his chest felt like a field of broken glass got married to a box of razor blades and the offspring sprouted in his lungs.

And there was an elephant standing on his head.

By the time Richie called him, he'd managed to drug himself enough to get out of the house, but Richie knew something was wrong. Lunch rolled around and all the drugs Skip took in the morning had a train wreck in his brain. Carpenter *drove* him home in the middle of the day because the Gentleman Caller called and Skip greeted him with "Tech's Teeth, how can it smell you?" and then put him on hold.

The nice secretary came clipping down the stairs a few moments later with strict instructions not to let Skipper come back to Tesko before Monday.

After driving him home, Carpenter helped him out of his clothes and into bed, laughing gently with him the whole time. "Do we like purple, Skip? What's our favorite color?"

"We like purple," Skip said, thinking that sounded like *genius* and wondering where his phone bank was. "But not as much as orange. Richie's hair is so... *orange*. We're sleeping together. Isn't that awesome?"

"Yeah, Skip. What's really awesome is that you wouldn't have told a soul if you weren't sick!"

"I'm *sick!*" Skip told him, horrified. He was bending over, trying to untie his shoes, and then he realized that he'd slid out of them as soon as they'd gotten through the door without letting Hazel out. "I'm *sick*, and Richie can't come until *Friday*." He paused, not sure if he and Carpenter had gotten this far. "I'm gay, Clay." He giggled. "Gay Clay. Good thing *you're* not gay, or that name would *stick!*"

Carpenter grunted. "Yeah, like I didn't hear *that* enough in grade school. But I'm glad to hear it from you. How's it feel?"

Skip tried to consider, but he was wobbling on his feet next to his bed. He liked his bed. It had brass rails on it. So shiny.

"Feels good," he said, trying to take the gay thing seriously. "Would feel better with Richie. *Everything* feels better with Richie."

Big broad hands maneuvered him until he was climbing into bed on all fours like a little kid. He got there, facing the far side, and then fell flat and wiggled until his head was up top and his feet were at the bottom.

"How's Richie feel about it?" Carpenter asked, covering him with his comforter.

"Richie hates it," Skip said glumly. "This blanket is so soft! I should get another one."

"I'll get it," Carpenter said, still so gentle. "Why does Richie hate it?"

"Richie likes *me!*" Skip clarified, his eyes closing. "But the gay thing is a scary word. Scary scary scary. Richie's dad is scary. His stepbrothers are scary. Me, I'm not scary. Don't want to be scary. It's all so...."

"Scary," Carpenter muttered, holding his hand to Skip's head. "Jesus, Skip, for as stoned as you are, you should not be this hot. Do you have a thermometer?"

"In the cupboard," Skip said.

"Frozen vegetables?"

"In the freezer. Why?"

"No reason. I'll panic after the thermometer."

Carpenter disappeared, and Skip lost time.

When he gained time, Carpenter and Richie were having a knockdown drag-out catfight in his kitchen.

Skip lay there in the peace of his bedroom and stroked Hazel, who was curling near his head without pets, so he *must* be sick.

"We're not putting frozen peas under his armpits!" Richie yelled. "And we're *not* taking him to the doctor's. That place probably made him sick in the first place."

"No, what made him sick in the first place was running around without a jacket in the rain, Richie. I'm telling you, 103 is a bad thing in an adult—"

"But not for Skip," Richie said, his voice coming down a little. "About three years ago he got sick and the guys from the soccer team came over and took turns with him. He told us he'd spiked fevers since he was a kid."

Oh yeah! "I'd forgotten that," Skip told Hazel. "They *were* here that time. That's nice. I mean, they won't come again, but it was nice of them to come that one time."

"What?" Richie said, coming in from the kitchen. "Skip, did you need anything?"

"I'd forgotten," Skip said simply, smiling at him. Oh, he looked good. His hair was in fabulous disarray from the rain, and he still had the metal brace on his nose, and the black eyes, but still, he looked like an angel from heaven. "I'd forgotten that the soccer team came over that time. I just remember lying here, feeling all alone." Everything hurt. His head, his joints, his throat, his ears. But Richie was *right there*. "Not all alone," he said, happy in spite of the misery. "You're here. And Carpenter too." He stroked Hazel. "Isn't that nice, Hazel?"

Hazel drooled and purred in one of her "Gee, it's good to be a house cat!" moments.

Richie came and sat next to Skip's bed and stroked back his sweaty hair. "You're really hot," he said quietly. "I can see why Carpenter freaked out. But the peas under the arms and the thighs— that's just...."

Skip shivered. "That would fuckin' *hurt*," he said with feeling. "Maybe just on the wrists. I think Jefferson did that. Was that Jefferson? Someone did that."

"That was me, you big moo," Richie said, laughing a little. "You... you kept asking for me. The guys figured since you and me were pretty tight, I should do most of the nursing. They didn't know I wanted you to notice me so bad."

Skip looked at him through sandy eyes. "I did," he assured. "I... I'd never been team captain before. You just kept telling everybody I could do it. I didn't want to let you down. That's how I became Skipper, I guess."

Richie leaned over and kissed his temple, worry clear on his face as he did so. "We'll put the frozen food on your wrists and ankles, 'kay?"

"You'll be nice to Carpenter, right?" Skip said anxiously. "He knows."

Yeah, that was right, wasn't it! Carpenter knew the big gay secret, and he didn't seem to care.

"He's pissed you didn't tell him earlier," Richie said, rubbing a rough thumb on Skip's jaw. "I tried to tell him we didn't know."

Skip suddenly wondered, in the strange lucidity of fever dream, how true that was.

"You ever think we knew?" he asked. "You ever think that just that once, we couldn't bear not knowing anymore?"

Richie closed his eyes and kissed Skipper's cheek. "Yeah, why not? I can't bear not knowing anymore. We'll go with that. Hang tight, Skip. We're going frozen food on your ass, okay?"

"Yeah. Thanks for the mushed-up peas...." Skip giggled to himself, and Richie sighed.

A few minutes later, Skip was just trying not to cry with the discomfort of that much cold on his wrists and ankles, and only the thought of that stuff shoved up in his armpits made him whimper and deal.

An hour later, his fever was down to 101.5, and Carpenter let out a ragged whoop of relief.

"That's awesome," he said, slumping down on a kitchen chair that he'd dragged into the bedroom. "Man, I saw us dragging him into the hospital and shit getting dire—"

"No hospitals," Skip said, remembering Richie's argument that he'd probably caught the bug while in the hospital. It was definitely possible. But worse than that.... "The guys would come visit in a hospital," Skip said, feeling lucid for the first time in two days. "And I apparently babble."

Next to him, Richie started to giggle. "Apparently babble? Is that what you said? You apparently babble?"

From his limp sprawl on the chair, Carpenter started to laugh too. "Yeah… did you hear that? He babbles! Who knew!"

Skip closed his eyes against them. "You two are making me tired," he said with dignity. And then he fell asleep.

He woke up in four hours, his fever spiking again, and Richie was there to give him meds and ice his extremities.

"Where's Carpenter?" Skip slurred. "Good guy. Needs to play soccer more often. You'll let him play soccer when they take me away, right?"

"Where you going?" Richie asked, sounding tired and distracted. Well, it *was* three in the morning. "And Carpenter went home. He'll be taking my spot in the morning."

"Mm…," Skip acknowledged. "And I'll be going to the gay league. They have to have a gay league for soccer, right? If they don't let us play in the rec league?"

Skip was lying on his back, the bags of vegetables on his wrists and ankles, while he stared at his ceiling and tried to make understandable patterns of his life from what he saw there.

Richie bustled around the room, cleaning the thermometer, replacing the tissues, grabbing the refillable water bottle, probably to fill it with water. He stopped all the activity to squint at Skipper.

"Why in the hell would *you* be going to a gay league when *I* would still be in rec league?" he asked.

Skipper gazed at him unhappily. All this time together and no sex. Being sick sucked. "Because I'm the one who outed us," he said, thinking it was reasonable. "I didn't mean to tell Carpenter. I don't want your dad to know and stop talking to you. I just want you to be able to stay during the week. So I get to go to gay league. Everyone at work knows I'm gay. You can stay in rec league. Nobody needs to know about you."

Richie shook his head. "Don't move," he muttered. He came back with a full bottle of cool water and more meds. "Here. Baby, sit up."

Skip complied and took the bottle of water and the meds. When he was done, he gratefully gave the bottle back to Richie, wondering if Richie was mad because he didn't want Skip to be in the gay league either.

"You at least want to be in the rec league still, right?" Skip asked mournfully after Richie was silent for a moment.

"I'll be in any league you are, Skip," Richie said wearily. "Gay league, rec league—you pick the game, I'll follow you on the field, okay?"

"I'm sorry I outed us to Carpenter. And the guy who wanted me to watch porn with him at work. And that guy's secretary."

Richie laughed a little and settled Skip down against the blankets again before turning off the light. "You know what I'm sorry for?"

"What?"

"That you're sick as a fucking dog. I'm fucking terrified for you, because you're actually sicker than you were three years ago. And you tried to drug yourself up and go to work like you didn't have any place better to go."

"That was dumb," Skip said, meaning it. He'd felt okay driving *to* work, but brother, about an hour after that, he'd been a *mess*.

"That was *lonely*," Richie said, his voice breaking. "And now you *should* be obsessing with getting better, and you're babbling about gay league soccer because you don't want to make me mad coming out. I'd stand up on the roof of our office and *blow you* if you'd just stop babbling enough to get better, okay, Skipper? Just… don't worry about gay league or rec league. You and me, we'll be you and me, and we'll play soccer, and it doesn't have to matter, okay?"

"But who's gonna come take care of me when you go?" Skip said, confused. "'Cause the team did it last time. But I babble."

"Me and Carpenter," Richie said. He made himself comfortable at Skip's back, but not touching. "We'll take care of you. Don't worry, Skip. You're not going to be left alone. And you know what? If we needed to, we'd call the team. If they didn't want to take care of you because of the gay thing, fuck 'em. We'll find other guys."

"*Like* our guys," Skipper said, feeling sullen. "Good guys."

"Yeah—they're only good if they treat you right. Now go to sleep, Skipper."

"Kk. Love you, Richie."

"Love you too, Skip."

"That gets easier to say every time."

"Yeah, I know. It's more important too, like, you know, brushing your teeth or coffee in the morning. Like you *have* to do it."

"Yeah." Skip smiled, his fever receding somewhat, his brain tired but sound for the first time in days. "Like drinking water or going to the bathroom. You can't think of it not happing."

"Or breathing, Skip. That sounds better."

"Yeah. Like breathing."

FUNNY THEY should mention that breathing was necessary. His fever died to manageable levels that night, but breathing became a happy memory, a thing of the past, as Skip's lungs filled up with crap that not even the most determined cough could keep out. He spent Wednesday and Thursday lying in bed limply, trying to expel his lungs through his open mouth by coughing. Richie stayed the night and Carpenter checked up on him during the day, and he almost wished they'd leave him alone. He always seemed to be making *the* most atrocious noises when they walked in.

Richie and Carpenter went to practice that night and told everybody Skip was sick but to practice anyway. Skip had written down a list of drills they should run, in succession, after they finished laps around the field.

Richie came back to the house and made sure he'd eaten soup and gave him a report on his guys.

"Carpenter was, like, poster child for working out—you should have seen him, Skip, running, doing the drills. I think he's lost weight, worrying about you."

Skip squinted at Richie, who still had the last vestiges of a nose brace on, as well as the two black eyes that came with it.

"I know how he feels," Skip muttered.

"Yeah, well, eat more than soup, or you're not going to fit into a thing you own. But you need to listen. The guys were real good—except for McAllister, but you know, he's always been sort of an asshole about 'Make me, whydoncha!' so that doesn't matter. They were good. They wanted to know if you're going to be there on Saturday and I said if you were, it was on the sidelines only."

"Aw," Skip said, and then coughed for ten minutes while Richie waited patiently for him to be able to finish his thought. "Maybe not," Skip managed to whisper when he was done. "Maybe sleeping without coughing—there's a priority."

Richie nodded. "I knew you were a smart man," he said with some satisfaction. He trailed a touch down the side of Skip's arm, and for the first time in days, Skip's body remembered what that meant.

"Ooh," he said, rolling over to face Richie. Richie had made him get up to change the sheets that morning, and he'd just showered and taken meds. If his chest hadn't felt shredded, he might have felt a light-year from sexy, instead of two or three galaxy lengths like he had been. "If I get better by Sunday, think you and me...." He batted his eyelashes, hoping that did it for Richie.

"I think we might," Richie said, rustling his hair. "But we gotta see if you can be a good boy being sick before you can be a grown-up getting well, 'kay, Skipper?"

"Best thing about being a grown-up is getting to have sex," Skip sulked.

Richie just laughed.

CARPENTER WAS there Friday while Richie went in and "pretended to work," as he said. Skip hadn't asked him what he was telling his dad this past week—he frankly didn't want to think about it. On the one hand, "My friend is sick and I'm helping" was a perfectly legitimate thing.

On the other hand, Skip wasn't sure if Richie was any better at secrets than Skip.

Carpenter wanted to weigh in on the matter as they played video games on the couch.

"If you had *Battlefield: Hardline*, Richie could tell his dad *that's* why he's coming over," he said while blasting through the latest-version *Witch Hunter* like he'd mastered it already. Because he had.

Skip watched his character die an ignominious death and sat back as Carpenter kept playing. He had to cough in a minute anyway. "I don't think a new video game ever kept anyone from suspecting gayness," he said matter-of-factly.

"I'm just saying, it would be a better excuse for him to be here."

Skip smiled weakly. "Would *you* like me to get *Battlefield: Hardline*, Carpenter?"

Clay shot him a shy smile. "Well, I *could* get it for you for Christmas. But you'd have to get me something cool too."

Skip laughed—and then coughed—and then laughed some more. "What should I get you that would make up for that?"

"Hm… how about coming to my parents' house for Thanksgiving in two weeks. Richie can come too if he wants, but you should definitely come."

Skip looked at him suspiciously. "Really?"

Carpenter won his level and hit Pause. "Yeah." He turned to Skip and handed him his slippery elm tea, which Skip was grateful for. "You're like my best friend, Skip—and obviously not the same way you and Richie have been best friends, okay? But my folks—and they mean well—they keep asking me about my social life and if I'm okay living away from home. You're a nice guy, you're reasonably well

99

adjusted, and when you're not sick, you actually make sense when you talk. It would be *great* if you could come over for Thanksgiving and convince Clyde and Cheryl Carpenter that their baby boy is not a complete social reject and that his last romantic breakup does not mean he's going to fester in his tiny apartment over Cheetos and Red Bull until his heart explodes."

Skip laughed, like he was supposed to, and then coughed for a good five minutes. He finished up and grimaced, because Carpenter was being very funny and very human—and not entirely truthful.

"You feel totally sorry for me," he said, feeling stupid when Carpenter grimaced in return.

"All that other stuff is true," he defended. "But… it didn't hit me until I drove you home, you know? You don't remember—you were giggling against the car window saying 'Whee!' the whole time. But I asked you why you even came into work. I mean, you had *permission* from one of the CEOs to stay home, and you come into your crappy IT job when you're wrecked like that?" Carpenter shifted on the couch and leaned on his elbows. "Do you know what you said?"

Skip's face heated. "Whee?" he guessed weakly.

"You said if Richie wasn't there, work was the only place you'd be missed."

Skip buried his face in his hands and looked wretchedly at the holey sweats, which were his *other* uniform from this horrible week because the non-holey (whole?) sweats were in the dryer. "I am now officially the most pathetic man alive," he muttered. "Please tell me you didn't say that to Richie."

The silence next to him was not encouraging.

"Carpenter!" Skip wailed. "I thought you were my *friend*!"

"I *am* your friend!" Carpenter held up his hands like he was defending himself. "I'm your friend, and I don't want you to be alone!"

"Yeah, because nothing says 'able to attract someone' like being so alone you're an object of pity! I mean how's he gonna…." Skip started to cough again, and this one was a doozy. But he was *thinking*: *How's he going to respect me enough to love me if he's sorry for me!*

100

"Richie fucking *reveres* you," Carpenter said when the coughing fit was over. "But I'd really love it if you came to my parents' for Thanksgiving. It would make both of us feel better."

Skip groaned and fell back against the couch cushions, suddenly too tired to even feel like shit. Richie's dad was doing Thanksgiving. Richie had said so the night before, after practice. Richie dreaded it—didn't like his stepmom's cooking, still hated his stepbrothers, and wasn't really fond of Kay's brother *or* his family—but he didn't want Skipper to come.

"I can go by myself and be miserable, or I could bring you and we could both be miserable. Seriously, Skipper—just watching you try not to hurl when they all start smoking in the house will make me feel like crap. You stay home and I'll come visit afterwards—or, even better, Friday morning, okay?"

Skip had nodded, exhausted and sad, and resigned himself to one more holiday alone.

Now he looked at Carpenter and actually felt a little bit of cheer starting. "Should I bring anything?" he asked hopefully.

"Bread. Remember when you made bread that once and brought it in? Make some more. It was really good."

Skipper thought about making bread and saving some for Richie. They could eat it the next day—in fact, he could make them a small chicken and some stuffing, without the nasty smoke residue.

That would work.

"Okay," he said, and for the first time since that first walk in the rain, he felt a little like himself. Richie would be there that night, and Skip would at least get to *see* the soccer game from the sidelines.

And he'd have Richie to himself for the rest of the weekend.

And in two weeks, he'd have a Thanksgiving with *someone's* family, even if it wasn't the one he'd hoped for.

RICHIE SHOWED up as promised, and although Skip was still sick, they had a delicious moment that night, both in their underwear, just touching *everything*. Richie turned in Skip's arms, his back to Skip's

101

front, and while Skip was rubbing his chest, his stomach, his throat, Richie stroked his own dick until his body tightened and he came.

His sexy little "Nung… nun-nunghhhh" was almost enough to make Skip hard through three layers of cold medicine too.

As it was, when Richie got back to bed after washing down, he nuzzled Skip's neck and kissed his cheek.

"I've never done that before," he said, and Skip managed to laugh without coughing.

"Beat off? Didn't you tell me you were going for some kind of record?"

Richie's laughter was much deeper, without the sodden edge of phlegm. "No—I mean in front of someone *else*."

"Yeah?" He felt some pride in that, and his melancholy over Thanksgiving started to fade.

"You're special, Skipper. Don't ever doubt it."

Skip fell asleep with his arm over Richie's tight stomach and had confused dreams about turkeys beating off and ejaculating gravy.

Fucking cold medicine.

Winning and Losing

SKIP BUNDLED up and wore his scarf and hat to the game, grateful it wasn't raining. Richie and Carpenter had both threatened to tie him to the bed if it was, and while from Richie this could have counted as something sexy and heretofore unexplored, from Carpenter it was spoken in sheer frustration.

The Scorpions played a team about equal to them, so Carpenter playing defender made a real difference in the rest of the team being able to play.

Skipper prowled the sidelines, unable to even shout directions, but every now and then Richie would look over at him and he'd point to someone and make gestures, and Richie would unerringly read his mind.

It seemed to be working too. The team had been pretty happy to see him (there'd been lots of backslapping and jokes about Kleenex), but once they got on the field, they were all business. Skip appreciated that about them—nobody asked once why they didn't get called into nursing duty again, and he wasn't sure how to explain, "I babble, and I finally have a secret worth telling."

They were tied 2-2 at the half, and Skip managed to give rusty directions when everybody came in for a drink of water and a huddle. When he was done telling McAlister to leave Carpenter alone because he was getting the job done, and Galvan and Owens to stop talking to each other in the midfield because the opposition was *listening* and figuring out what they were doing, he called "Break!" and sent them all back on their way. They had just finished the kickoff when a couple of not-quite-familiar people wandered down on the field.

Oh fuck.

They were actually *wandering* onto the *field*.

Skip had managed to avoid shouting for half a soccer game, but he sucked in a breath and hollered, "Get off the field, we're *playing* here!"

He doubled over to cough after that, but as he was going down, he recognized the startled face that turned toward him.

Oh hell.

A few minutes later the two people who'd hurriedly run off the field to circle round the back drew near him, and he had to fight not to wheeze when the smell of cigarette smoke hit him.

"Hi, Mr. Scoggins," he said weakly, holding out a hand.

To his relief, Richie's dad took his hand and shook it, and his stepmom gave Skipper a rather reserved nod from behind his shoulder.

"Good to see you up and about, Skip," Ike Scoggins said, his voice measured.

The day was blustery and cold, and Skipper felt his cheeks heat under that even look. "Yeah, well, Richie and Carpenter wouldn't let me play." Skip hoped he was being charming. "They said after all that work getting me better, if I wrecked myself playing rec league ball, they'd strangle me."

Those had been Carpenter's words, actually. *Richie's* words had been "For the love of Christ, if you love me at all, you'll just get fucking better."

"Well, maybe now that you're better, Richie can stop spending all his time at your place," Ike said, and Skip shrugged.

"We play video games," he said. "Carpenter too. When the weather gets better, they're going to help me fix the yard up so I can get a dog."

His yard was already fixed up—but he was dying here, under that nicotine-scented breath and even stare. Ike Scoggins looked a lot like Richie—narrow cheekbones, bony jaw, redhead's coloring, except Ike's skin was cooked a darker red than Richie's. But he was missing the bright eyes and the potential for laughter. And the gentleness that sometimes took Skip's breath away.

"You seem to rely an awful lot on the kindness of strangers," Kay said, her voice derisive. "Someday you're going to have to stand on your own."

"Like Paul and Rob?" Skip asked acidly. He knew very well they both lived *in* the house with Ike and Kay, while Richie paid rent to live over the garage and pretend he had his own life.

"Decent apartments are hard to come by," Kay snapped, and Skip wanted to reply *They are with what you pay!* but his team needed him.

The turnover was that quick—just long enough for a conversation with two people who appeared to hate Skipper's guts—but suddenly the other team had the ball and they were making inroads against the Scorpions' weakest link.

"Carpenter! Back up closer to the goal and use your body!" Skip hollered, and Carpenter nodded but didn't look up. Good guy. Smart player. Would get faster in time.

"You really trusting that fat guy to be a defender?" Ike asked, and Skip fought to not punch him in the nose.

"That guy just took care of me for a week when I didn't know what day it was," Skip muttered. "You show some fucking respect to my players." He raised his voice then. "Cooper, get in there and be his backup! Jefferson, be ready for Cooper's play—" Cough hack blargh.

He ignored everything and everybody then in an effort to breathe, and when he came up for air, his team had the ball again and Richie and McAlister were moving forward. "Go, Richie, go!" Skip croaked, and Richie didn't look up either, but he *did* do exactly the play he and Skip used to do. He kicked it to McAlister right before the defender moved back so McAlister could punch it forward.

And McAlister turned around and passed it back, but they'd moved past the defender at that point and offsides it was.

"McAlister, you asshole," Skip muttered. "You just had to kick it into the goal. He *gave* that to you."

McAlister turned to Skip and held up his hands in the classic "my bad" shrug, and Skip gave him back some.

The look Richie gave him was much more to the point, and Skip was glad they didn't have any locks of McAlister's reddish hair around, or there would have been voodoo dolls all over Skip's house. Then Richie saw his parents, and the profound look of disgust and irritation that crossed his face could be read across the field and then some.

"He doesn't look happy to see us," Kay said, but she sounded like this thrilled her no end. Skip would have given anything at that point to get into his car and drive home and get back into bed with Hazel, but he didn't even have his car there—he'd come with Richie.

"He wasn't expecting an audience," Skip said, trying to be gracious. The other guys brought wives and girlfriends sometimes, but not always. Mostly this was just something that they *did*, and the pizza and beer afterward were like their dues into an exclusive little social club of shared interest and friendships that did not run the risk of becoming what Richie, Carpenter, and Skip had become: entangled.

"He used to beg me to come see him do shit," Ike said, sounding sad. For a moment Skipper felt bad—he glanced up, thinking he could say something comforting, and then realized that if he said one half of what he knew Richie felt about his dad, that would be too much info for him to have.

"He's just surprised," Skipper did say, his voice weak.

And then the team needed him and he ignored Richie's parents because he couldn't change them.

They ended up losing, but the team made him feel better by saying that was because they needed him on the field and in full lung capacity. He laughed, and there was a lot of good-natured ribbing about him singing "Whee!" all the way home from work on Tuesday, and then Owens called time.

"Skip, we're glad you could come—but dude. You look wiped. Let Scoggins take you home and feed you soup or something, okay?"

At that point Richie's dad spoke up. "You're staying at Skip's again, Richie?"

Skip watched as the attention of the entire team focused in on Richie's face, and his green eyes grew really big. Awesome.

"Yeah, well, Dad, I sort of drove him here."

"You gonna be back tonight?" Kay demanded. "I was going to cook."

Skip wanted to cry. He watched his boyfriend go from a triumphant adult to a called-out little kid in about two seconds.

"We'll see," he said. "Depends on if Skip's okay or not. How you doin', Skip?"

Skip saw Carpenter staring at him like "Do something, dammit," so he obliged.

He promptly launched into a coughing fit so brutal it made him throw up.

By THE time they cleared his front door, he could almost breathe again, and Richie hadn't stopped apologizing.

"I'm so sorry," he said for the umpteenth time as he opened the door. He had his own set of keys now, which was sort of wonderful, but it didn't make this moment any better. "Man, I should have just told them. I mean, right then and there, you know? Just said, 'Staying the night at a friend's, you got a problem with that?' But all the guys were looking at me, and all I could think about was how much I wanted this weekend, you know?"

Skip's throat was done. He couldn't make a sound if his house was on fire. But his Richie-defense system worked just fine.

He closed the door behind him and reached out and snagged Richie by the hood of his windbreaker.

Richie whirled and looked at him, leaning against the door and smiling weakly.

"What?" he asked suspiciously.

Skip pointed to his throat and shrugged. He'd actually *tried* to get a word in edgewise in the car, but all that came out was wind. It sounded like he was whispering to himself.

"You can't talk now?" Richie asked, sounding like this was the last straw.

Skip shook his head and mouthed, "Nope."

107

"Well hell! My dad's suspicious, he practically made me out the two of us to the whole ball club, and you have laryngitis? What are we supposed to do now?"

Skip made a big puckered-lipped kissy face, and Richie cracked up.

"No," he said, laughing. "You have luggage under your eyes I could ship somewhere special, like New York. No kissing for you."

Skip raised his eyebrows and tried his best puppy-dog face. "Soup?" he mouthed.

Richie chuckled weakly and walked into his arms. "Sure," he said quietly. "I'll make you some soup. You go lie down and I'll get busy. Me and Carpenter bought you groceries Thursday night. I think I could make a really tasty soup."

Skipper mimed wielding a can opener. Then he circled his arms and made more kissy faces.

Richie pecked him on the lips. "You have a one-track mind, Skipper. No. I'm going to make you some really good soup, and I'm going to take care of you right. If my folks are going to get all weird and into my personal business, I'm going to make this count."

Skip sighed heavily and crossed his arms. "Can I have a cookie after the soup?" he wheezed.

Richie reached up and cupped his cheek. "You managed to talk me down and out of the tree, Skipper. You can have anything you want."

Skip smiled and nuzzled his palm and allowed himself to be shooed off to bed.

But inside he was thinking that there was trouble brewing from Richie's parents, from the team, from the whole world that he wasn't going to be able to put off, and maybe Richie wasn't ready to face.

God. He was actually *grateful* for the fucking plague. At least that gave him a reason to postpone real life for another week, maybe two. They could do this until after Thanksgiving, right?

THAT EVENING he watched, after being ordered helplessly to the couch, while Richie ran around and swept, vacuumed, and dusted.

"I'm not helpless!" he protested, but his voice still hadn't come back, and Richie assured him he looked like a television with the sound off. Finally he just accepted the help and leaned his chin on his fist, watching television. When Richie was done scrubbing the bathroom, he took a quick shower and came back into the living room to sit next to Skip and watch some TV.

After about half an hour of silence and gentle touches, Richie hit Pause on the television and started talking, still staring ahead like there was something on.

"Carpenter told me you're going to Thanksgiving with him. That's fine—I mean, I can't, and I guess it's okay. But I mean, I think with someone else, they'd assume you couldn't fall in love with Carpenter because he's a big guy, but I know you. You got a big heart. So even though he's straight and that couldn't really happen, I want you to know that it's just like when Kay tried to set me up with a girl. I don't like it. Okay?"

"Okay," Skip whispered. "Anything else?"

Richie turned to him and frowned, then did that thing where he stroked Skip's cheek. At first Skip had thought it was just a one-time thing, or because he was sick, but now he was realizing that was Richie's *thing*—that was where he touched when he wanted reassurance.

So sweet.

"Yeah. But I don't got words for it. Just... just I wish next weekend was already here. I mean, tomorrow is going to be long, and I'll leave Monday morning, but suddenly I'm all afraid of leaving you alone."

"Not sick anymore," Skip rasped, and Richie rolled his eyes.

"That's bullshit, clear and simple. But it's more than just the sick and being too stupid to stay home. It's that you didn't think you had anybody if you stayed home."

"Know different now." Skip indulged himself in shimmying his hand under Richie's sweatshirt. Ah, skin. He loved the silky feel of the skin at Richie's hip.

Amy Lane

"Do you?" Richie asked, clearly still worried. "You promise you'll reach out to someone if you're sick or hurt or your car breaks down—"

"Auto service," Skip teased.

Richie scowled, not amused. "You know what I mean!"

Skip stroked Richie's stomach before slipping his hand up to pinch his nipples. Richie's indrawn breath was *so* worth it. "I'll call you," he whispered. "Do you want to be my calling person? I'll make you my calling person."

"More than that!" Richie's voice broke with a particularly hard pinch. "Stop that, Skipper!" He batted at Skip's hand, but Skip slid it down to the waistband of his sweats first.

"What's more?" Skip asked, distracting him.

"Be honest," Richie breathed. "*Skip!*"

Skip slid his hand under Richie's boxers and started to tease the fattening length of Richie's cock. He was tired of being lectured on how he needed to take care of himself. He wanted to touch Richie naked!

"How's this for honest?"

Richie arched his back and thrust into Skip's palm, and Skip took the invitation, wrapping his fingers around Richie's cock and squeezing. "Not what I'm... oh Jesus, Skipper, what are you—"

Skip slid Richie's sweats all the way down his hips and knelt before him, suddenly tired of being tired and achy and sore. Dammit, he *wanted*, and he wanted more than just to tease. He couldn't contribute to the conversation, but he could damned well contribute to the company.

He squeezed Richie's cock from base to tip and then popped the tip in his mouth and began to stroke.

"We will—" Richie's voice broke as Skip stopped just shy of bottoming out and swallowed to ease his throat. "Have this...." Skip pulled up and licked quickly around Richie's cockhead. "Discussion...." And down almost to the bottom again. Skip slid his hand between Richie's legs and fondled his balls.

110

"*Later!*" Richie moaned, giving up and slowly, carefully fucking Skip's mouth. Skip squeezed and slurped and licked and stroked, and Richie dragged his hands through Skip's hair.

Skip relaxed into it, wondering when being on his knees in front of Richie with Richie's cock in his mouth had become a comfort area. It *was* a comfort. Not so much Richie's taste (since he couldn't really taste much anyway) but the feeling of his flesh, solid and real, and the noises he made, and, most importantly, that Skip was the center of his world.

Richie's movements became more frantic, and his hips started to jerk in little spasms, and Skip devoted all his concentration to driving Richie wild. He used to beat off three times a day, right? Well here was a guy, his mouth open, his fist engaged, just dying for... just begging for....

Richie knotted his fingers in Skip's hair (which was getting long) and pulled his head back. "I'm gonna come," he whispered, massaging his fingers against Skip's scalp. "No swallowing. You'll be coughing jizz for a week."

Skip opened his mouth and balanced Richie's cock on his tongue, his lips pulled back in a smile. He just held there, bouncing his tongue up and down, up and down, until Richie arched and thrust, calling out, "God, Skipper, you *suck!*"

And then Skipper *did* suck, and he sucked hard, and Richie spilled hot and bitter into his mouth, the first thing he'd actually tasted in a week.

Of course he swallowed.

Richie continued to pump weakly, like he couldn't help it, and when he gave a final shudder and sat still, Skip slurped him off one final time to make sure he was all sparkly clean.

Richie glared at him with a certain grim humor, even as Skip fussed with his sweats and pulled them back up and straightened his shirt so it looked like he'd just been sprawled in front of the couch watching television, and hadn't been getting a blow job at all.

"This changes nothing," Richie said, trying hard to maintain the soberness that had claimed him *before* the blow job.

Skip grinned, all teeth, and Richie broke character and laughed, ruffling his hair.

"Okay, fine. I'm not as uptight as I was twenty minutes ago. But I still want you to call me if anything goes wrong. Don't try to blow sunshine up my ass; don't tell me it's all fine when you're too sick to move. Don't… don't pretend you're not alone for my sake, Skipper. I get to be the one person in the world—and that includes Carpenter—who makes you not alone anymore."

Skip's grin softened, and he rested his temple against Richie's thigh. He held up his hand then, looking at Richie hopefully, and Richie tangled fingers with him.

"Yeah," Richie said, squeezing a little. "We're like that."

Skip's smile deepened and he returned the squeeze. Yes, yes they were.

THE NEXT day he could actually talk—hurray!—and Richie was less inclined to lecture and more inclined to make love.

Which they did.

A *lot*.

The second time, Skip took Richie while he was plastered up against the headboard, hands clutching the rail, the bed rocking so loud they probably couldn't have heard a bomb go off. Richie was screaming, "Fuck me! Fuck me, Skip! Fuck me!" and Skip's cock, finally free of the constraints of cough syrup and painkillers, was fucking like a released prisoner would fly.

Richie's head lolled back on Skip's shoulders, his hair a glorious autumn-colored spill against Skip's pale skin, and Skip could look down at his ginger-furred freckled body, and he wanted it, craved it, couldn't fuck it enough. Richie's stout cock kept knocking against the rails as Skip pounded, and every time it did, he let out a keen of ultimate arousal, a sort of plea for even more, and Skip obliged.

But Skip needed to come—and *soon*—or his newly healing body was going to give up on him, so he rasped, "Fuck your fist, Richie. C'mon, squeeze it hard. Want to see you—"

Oh, that was all it took. Pump, pump, and white jizz spewed from the end of his cock and all over the pillows, the rails, the walls. Richie sagged in his arms, and Skipper shivered, turned on by everything from the clench of Richie around his cock to the sight of Richie's come running off the brass rail of the bed.

"Nungh.... Augh!"

It had been a while. This orgasm didn't roll, it ripped, split him open from groin to chin, shot him through with white light, spilled his insides clean into Richie, gave them to Richie to keep, deep inside his body.

He and Richie puddled to the bed like melted butter, both of them sweating in the chill.

"Skip?" Richie panted after a few moments of silence.

"Yeah?"

"I think we're getting better at this."

"I know something's getting better," Skip said, his voice sandy but there.

"I don't want to wait until—"

The pounding at Skip's door took them both by surprise.

In the mad scramble that followed, Skip found himself wearing his one clean pair of sweats, commando, and Richie's hooded sweatshirt without a shirt on underneath. It was tight across his chest and left his stomach bare.

"Go!" Richie commanded, turning on the television loud. He ran to the vaporizer in the corner of the room, and Skip didn't hang around to see what he was doing next, because the pounding on the door hadn't stopped.

He got to the door and swung it open, and almost choked on his tongue when he saw Richie's dad.

Oh holy fucksticks on crackers. How loud had they been? How did he look? Had he smeared jizz through his hair as they'd been running around?

"Mr. Scoggins," he said, his voice rasping and catching. "What're you doin' here?"

"Here to see if Richie's ready to come home yet," Ike said, glaring at him.

Skip smiled back, hoping he didn't look like the guy who'd been fucking Ike's baby boy into the mattress five minutes earlier.

"I'm not sure—he was planning to go shopping a little later," Skip said. Shopping for Thanksgiving decorations—so domestic, like real boyfriends, but he wasn't going to tell that to Richie's dad.

"He's buying your *food*?" Ike's mouth pulled up into a sneer, and Skip decided not to let him in.

"He eats here too," he said, his voice extra raspy. At that moment, whatever Richie had been doing with the vaporizer rolled through the living room, and Skip's head felt clear for the first time that day, and Richie's dad started to cough up a lung.

"What—" Cough, cough, cough. "—in the *fuck* is that?"

"Mentholyptus," Skip said, taking some more deep breaths. "Wow. That shit works *awesome*."

At that moment Richie came out of the bedroom wearing Skip's work sweatshirt and his jeans, but barefoot.

"Dad?" he asked, sounding for all the world like his father wouldn't notice they were wearing each other's clothes. "I told you I'd be at work Monday morning."

"Richie, what in the hell are you doing here—"

"Yeah, sorry about the Vicks VapoRub stuff. I put way too much in the humidifier—that was *not* what I meant to happen."

"Are you kidding? That was *great!*" Skip was really very grateful. It was like he had full use of his senses for the first time in *forever*.

"Yeah?" Richie grinned at him, and for a moment they could pretend like they hadn't almost gotten busted having ass sex in the bedroom of Skip's tiny house. "I'll remember that."

"You need to come home right now," Ike snarled, and Richie's happy little bounce deflated.

"No," he said quietly. "Sorry, Dad. I mean, I don't have any family stuff, and my time is my own, right?"

"Not to spend it doing...." Ike glared at them both, as though daring them to find the right words.

"Doing what?" Skip asked, voice husky but firm. "What is it you think we're doing, sir? Richie and I have been friends for years—what are you seeing here that's bad?"

"Don't bullshit with me, young man," he snarled. "You two—this ain't right. You can't get away with what you're doing—someone'll stop you!"

He turned away then and stalked toward his car, leaving Richie and Skip shaking as they closed the door behind him.

"Oh Jesus," Skip said, leaning against the door. "Did Hazel get out?"

"No. She's hiding under the bed. Skip, did you hear him?" Richie was leaning against the door too, their arms touching.

"Yeah—I just don't know who he thinks is going to stop us," Skip muttered, looking at Richie with wide eyes. "I mean... he's not going to *do* anything, is he?"

"You mean like sabotage your car or burn down your house?" Richie asked seriously.

"The fact that's where your mind goes is really frightening. *Will* he?"

Richie shook his head. "No. No, I don't think so. But... but Rob and Paul might not be so smart. Jesus, Skip. I should go—"

"No," Skip said, his eyes suddenly burning. "No. What's going to happen? You go home and say, 'Sorry, Dad, you're right, I *won't* go play at Skip's again?' What happens to soccer? What happens to *us*? Are you ready to walk away from that yet?"

Richie grabbed his hand and clung. "No," he said softly. "No. You're right. We'll go shopping like we planned. Buy some of those eucalyptus arrangements for your table so we don't have to dump menthol all over the bedroom. God, I can't believe that doesn't bother you."

"Best my head's felt in a week," Skip confirmed. "But we should probably get out of here anyway." Skipper straightened up and felt his junk flopping around in his sweats and the cold air hitting his stomach. "But first...."

"Yeah. We totally need to change."

RICHIE LEFT Monday morning again, and this time they kissed at the door for as long as they possibly could before both of them would be late.

When they broke it off, Richie was mashed up against the door and Skip was holding his thighs as he wrapped his legs around Skip's waist. They paused for a moment, leaning foreheads together, and gulped air.

"What do I tell my dad?" Richie asked.

"Tell him you're in love."

"I'm so in love with you," Richie told him, burying his face in Skip's shoulder. Skip held him one more second, then another, then let him go.

Thankful

THE NEXT week seemed so blessedly normal.

Work was fine—the fruit basket from Mr. Gentleman Caller was much appreciated, and Skip and Carpenter got a lot of use from it. The card read *Thanks for not suing for sexual harassment. I hope your boyfriend took good care of you.*

Skip and Carpenter toasted to a new friend with big Japanese pears that tasted like heaven itself—and Skip took a page from his nearly forgotten youth and sent an actual handwritten thank-you card when he was done.

The rain let up for a week, leaving them with mist and fog, but since that was normal November weather, it didn't hardly get Skip down. He and Richie texted almost once an hour, and Skip started playing Words With Friends with him, not because either of them was a better-than-average player but because it meant once an hour he had an excuse to let Richie know Skip was thinking about him.

Once an hour, Richie did the same thing. (And Richie was particularly adept at finding the dirty word in his stack of tiles, a gift that never ceased to amaze Skipper. The word "vulva" actually won the game for him on Wednesday, and Skipper was full of praise.)

Richie showed up for soccer about half an hour late, though, and although Skip wasn't going to yell at him—because he wouldn't anyway—at the end of the game, he did use the excuse to call him over to help pick up the orange cones so they could talk about why he was late.

Winter ball practice was at Rusch Park instead of the middle school, because the park had lights, and they were two of the last people there, moving slowly, their silence companionable. They met at the end of the field, and Skip gathered the cones and started moving to their cars. The parking lot was decently lit, especially from the

117

practice lights, and if their breath hadn't been steaming as they spoke, it might have been a nice place for a nighttime chat. As it was, Skip told Richie to get in and he'd drive him to his car at the far end of the parking lot, and Richie slid in gratefully.

"Sorry, Skip," he said as soon as he shut the door. "My dad—I mean, it's been lots of little stuff, you know? He's been knocking on my door at night like he's tucking me in. Paul and Rob suddenly found Jesus, and it's all about what Jesus would do to a fag on a dark night—"

Skip grunted. "Okay, they are about the two dumbest assholes on the planet. I mean, four years ago people bought that shit, but hasn't everybody figured out that Jesus was gay-friendly by now?"

Richie grinned at him. "Oh, I told 'em. Quote chapter and verse—"

"You know your Bible that well?" Because that was something they had *not* covered in their late-night conversations.

"Naw, I know my *gay* that well," Richie corrected, nodding. "I've got a laptop—I've been looking shit up. I mean, I know you were down last week, but you said the magic word, Skipper. You said 'gay' and I had a thing to research, and now I know my gay Bible stuff and Rob and Paul can kiss my ass."

Skip laughed as he pulled up next to Richie's car and put it in park, letting it idle.

"That's awesome," he said, meaning it. Then he sobered. "So I guess we're in gay league soccer together if the guys find out, right?"

Richie sighed and leaned his head against Skip's shoulder. "Yeah. Well, there's worse things than not playing winter ball, Skipper. Do you want to just up and tell them? I mean...." He dropped a kiss on Skip's collarbone, and Skip nuzzled his temple. "Carpenter surprised me, you know? Your job surprised me. My dad even—he knows. I mean, there was not enough eucalyptus in the *world* to disguise the way your house smelled on Sunday, and he keeps acting surprised when he comes over to my place, like he's expecting a big gay orgy. But he's got to know. What happens if we just say it and... and...."

118

Skip turned his head and saw Richie looking at him with wide, limpid eyes, begging Skip for something.

Skip didn't like making Richie beg. He kissed him then, openmouthed, and Richie sighed and sank into it. Urgent but contained, because they weren't going to get laid in Skip's car—they could wait until the weekend for that.

But still passionate. Still the taste of Richie's mouth in his own. Still the acknowledgment, somehow, that what started out in Skip's car and had raged uncontrollably had now turned into something other than fire. It had transformed *them*, and they needed to see who they were.

They were the same two guys who had met at tech school and who had grown progressively closer ever since. They were the same two guys who had discovered their first real sex and their first kiss and their first love in each other's arms.

Skip pulled back after a few moments, knowing his cock was swollen but feeling the weight of being a grown-up. "After Thanksgiving," he said, while Richie blinked around like he was trying to figure out which day it was.

"What?"

"After Thanksgiving. We've got practice Friday afternoon. I'll tell everyone then. I'll just tell 'em I'm gay if you want. If they get ugly, I'll leave you out of—"

"Oh fuck *that*, Skipper," Richie snapped, shaking his head. "You think I don't know what you're risking? You're risking your... your family unit here—"

"And so are you," Skip said gently. Richie's hair was growing long too, and Skip wound a sweaty ringlet around his finger. "Your dad already—"

"You know the saddest thing about my dad right now?" Richie said, voice hard.

"What?"

"He doesn't have anything to hold over me, Skip. He doesn't have a single thing I want. There is nothing he can threaten me with that will make me change what I feel when I'm with you."

119

Skip smiled, a sort of serenity seeping through his chest. "Okay, then," he said, dropping a kiss on Richie's forehead. "We're the family we each need. That's… that's something I can live with."

It felt good then, right? Felt hopeful.

The next morning Richie called Skip from work to say the junkyard had been completely vandalized. Cars had been torched, their best stock had been put into the masher—it was a mess, and Richie's dad had everybody working overtime until they had a quote for the insurance people.

So no Richie that weekend, no sex, no warmth, and definitely no plans for coming out.

Skip just had to buckle down for a long, lonely weekend and look forward to Thanksgiving with Carpenter's parents instead.

CARPENTER WASN'T having any of that bullshit.

"Not for the whole weekend?" he said when Skip explained it to him at lunch. Carpenter was moving much more quickly now, so they actually had more time to talk during lunch. Skip didn't know if it was okay to say how proud he was, but it was true. His friend had really taken to the soccer thing, had been working out on his own since Halloween—at least Skip suspected so.

"It's his dad's livelihood," Skipper said glumly. He'd gotten soup today, but it did not seem to be doing its job in comforting him. "And Richie's starting to suspect that it's more than just vandalism." Richie'd texted right before lunch, saying he was pretty sure all of the prime parts of their best stock had been missing before the car bodies had been crushed. "It was like all the valuable stuff had been taken out before it got destroyed. And the alarms hadn't gone off, and they should have been working."

"So this is a really big deal," Carpenter said, sounding relieved.

Skip glanced up and smiled wanly. "Yeah, he's not just trying to ditch me."

"You sound worried."

"His dad…."

"Yeah—I saw he showed up at the game. Didn't seem…."

"Warm," Skipper said. That was the operative word right there. Richie's family wasn't warm. "And he hates my suddenly gay ass like you can't believe." Was that getting easier to say? Skip thought that maybe since he and Richie were both saying it, it felt like it fit. A little part of him wondered, *Is this why I didn't say it before? Is this why Richie didn't? Because we were afraid of saying it alone?*

"I caught that," Carpenter said, furry eyebrows raised dryly. "Nice move, throwing up on the field, by the way. I think all gay men should use that to avoid coming out of the closet."

Skipper covered his eyes with his palm. "Yeah. That was classy, right? Way for Skip to be a stand-up guy."

"Hey, Richie wasn't ready. *I* could see it. And nobody wants to say something personal on the soccer field. It's why men bond over sports, for Christ's sake."

Skip nodded and straightened in his seat, trying to concentrate on his soup. "Still. Richie keeps saying he can do it all himself, but…." Skip slurped meditatively and swallowed. His chest was still a little raw, and the liquid soothed.

"But…."

"But I thought I was okay when I was sick," Skip said, still sort of embarrassed. "But I was lucky that cough medicine didn't kick in when I was driving. And if you and Richie hadn't taken care of me, I'd probably be dead and Hazel would be eating my face right now."

With a look of disgust, Carpenter put down the rest of his turkey avocado sandwich. "That's awesome. It's not bad enough you've got me playing soccer and working out and eating healthy, now you want me to *hate* food too?"

"No—forget the part about the cat. The point is that I needed people. I needed you and Richie, and maybe I should have admitted it sooner, but I'm admitting it now. But I wouldn't have if Richie hadn't tried to get me to promise I'd never try to curl up and die on my own again."

"He's a good boyfriend," Carpenter said, going back to the turkey avocado with gusto. "And your point is?"

"That he might need a little help with talking to his dad. Not this weekend, though. This weekend, he's busy." And Skip was back to feeling glum and cheated.

"Oh hell no." Carpenter threw the last of the sandwich in his mouth. "If you've got nothing to do this weekend, you *owe* me."

"Owe you...." Skip eyed him suspiciously. "What do you need?"

"I need a golfing buddy," Carpenter said. "Seriously. Couple of times a year my high school gang goes golfing and compares conquered worlds. I go. I hate it. And I always have nothing to say. I mean, they've all graduated from college—"

"As have you," Skip felt compelled to point out. Unlike Skip, Carpenter had a bachelor's degree in computer science and not a tech certificate. Skip got the feeling that Carpenter was teching his way through Tesko because it was easy and nobody expected anything from him, which was demoralizing in its way. Having a job with benefits had been Skip's *dream*. Well, until he'd kissed Richie—now he had another one.

"Yeah, well, they're doing something with their degrees, they're making lots of money doing it, and they're smug bastards about it."

This sounded like so much fun Skip would rather be sick. "And you want me to come because...."

"Because you're the most interesting thing that I've got in my life."

Skip gaped at him in horror. "Oh, Carpenter...."

"Yeah, I know. Pathetic. But also true. You can come and be a gay soccer coach—I'll get to fly my liberal flag, because most of them are as conservative as the diamonds shoved up their asses, and you and I can talk about whether or not *Assassin's Creed Syndicate* actually redeemed the shitty last version."

"Mn," Skip hedged, because he hadn't been convinced, but all the gamer magazines were saying it was the next best thing.

"Yeah, right? I mean we could spend the whole day talking about that. And Skip...." Carpenter smiled like he was enticing a kid with a piece of candy. "Ski-ip... it's *voluntary exercise*."

Skip laughed a little. "You've been exercising off the soccer field—you can't fool me. You're looking real good."

"Yeah, well, that was because I thought I was gonna die after that first practice. I can't promise it will stick, though. So yeah? Since you and Richie don't have the weekend together, I get to have you for golf?"

Well, what could he say? The guy had just helped nurse him back to health.

"Yeah, but I warn you. Richie gets jealous—this whole thing better suck and we need to bitch loudly about it, or he's gonna wanna take you out."

Carpenter laughed then—a real laugh—and Skip felt marginally better. Richie had been right about everybody needing people. He was glad to be one of Carpenter's people.

Fore!

CARPENTER'S FRIENDS were everything Carpenter was not. They showed up to the course in Fair Oaks in designer golfwear plaid pants and pastel polos, which Skip tried not to smirk at. He and Carpenter were in khakis and hooded sweatshirts—in Carpenter's case, khaki cargo shorts, in spite of the brisk wind. Skip had asked about dress codes, but Carpenter had just smirked and showed his ID and they hadn't gotten more than a look as they'd entered the club.

Carpenter's friends talked about their stock portfolios, how they were getting their MBAs in marketing or their law degrees to facilitate their next promotion, and how they were spending their Thanksgiving weekend going to fundraisers their parents were sponsoring.

Oh. And whether Corfu was a better vacation spot than Santorini.

Austen Mathers, the queen bee—erm, primary captain of the universe—did his condescending best to pull Skip into the conversation right when he was fixing to swing at the ball.

"So, uhm, *Skip*, where's *your* favorite place to vacation?"

"Disneyland," Skip said promptly. What had it been—two years ago? Skip, Richie, Jefferson, and Thomas had all gone down to Anaheim and roomed in the Tropicana. A five-star resort? No. But it had been *across the street* from Disneyland, and they'd gotten the three-day pass. For three days Skip had ridden all the rides, shaken hands with all the characters, waved at all the happy children, and basically relived a part of his crappy childhood but did it better. He still had the autograph book with pictures of him and the guys with as many characters as they could find. Jefferson had been on board with the character worship, but Richie? Richie had been right next to Skip in the front of the line. Thomas had humored the three of them—they knew that—but Skip and Richie? Skip had looked through that book a couple of times since then. Jefferson had looked happy, Thomas had looked long-suffering—but that look on his and Richie's faces was as enchanted as any child's. That book, that time, that was important to them.

"Disneyland." Austen smirked and Skip nodded seriously.

"Swear to God, it's the happiest place on earth. Now hang on here, I gotta swing." This was the first time Skip had played golf— Carpenter had brought him his dad's set of clubs so he didn't have to rent any, claiming it was a fair swap for the soccer equipment Skip had lent him. He'd been five over par on the first hole—he wasn't sure if that was called a bogey or a booger or a giant fucking dump—but he'd spent the round studying Carpenter's friends and their swings, and their approach to the ball and the stick and the hole. He was pretty coordinated, and good at watching and learning and applying. Hell, it was how he'd faked a social life since the sixth grade.

Okay, back straight, knees bent, arms not locked, club as a giant lever, applying force right....

There.

Skip and Carpenter watched in awe as the ball arched, arched, arched, and fell, about four feet from the cup.

"Holy shit," Carpenter breathed. "Skip, are you serious?"

"Apparently so," Skip said, grinning at him. "Now all I gotta do is figure out how to punt."

"Putt," Carpenter smirked.

"Yeah, whatever."

Austen—who had *barely* done better than Skip at the last hole— was glaring at him with a locked jaw. "That was pretty lucky," he said through gritted teeth. "Good luck doing that again."

To Carpenter's delight, he did. And to Skip's surprise, Carpenter was pretty damned good too.

"I get it now," Skip said as the two of them were walking ahead of the group to the next hole.

"Get what?" Carpenter said innocently before taking a swig of his flavored water.

"I was wondering—why would my good buddy Carpenter, who's sort of awesome, be hanging out with those pricks every year."

"Yeah?" Oh, that smirk through all that fuzz on his cheeks did *not* get any less charming. Skip could totally see why Carpenter could get women, extra weight and slacking notwithstanding. Not that Richie had anything to worry about, but it made Skip root for his friend.

"You wipe the fucking floor with them—"

"And my dad's the one who gets us the tee time," Carpenter gloated.

"Oh dear Lord." They were coming up to the next group of people playing the hole, and they propped their bags up at a polite distance and talked companionably.

"Dear Lord what?" Carpenter asked.

"This is just mean. You didn't even *need* me—you could have lorded your superiority over them without me."

Carpenter's laughter was low and cruel. "Yeah, but you make it even *better*. You're good-looking, you're gay, and you just *totally* destroyed them in a game they've gotten lessons in for years."

Skip grunted. "You didn't know I was going to do that," he pointed out uncomfortably. "What if I'd sucked?"

Carpenter shrugged. "See, in the first place, I didn't see that happening. And in the second place, it would have been good too, because you and me could be talking about things like gay rights and marriage equality while we were right in the middle of them. It would have been *great*."

"I feel a little used," Skip said, although from a snarky bastard perspective, that could have been fun.

"Yeah, well, don't. I'm just as happy we got to play through. You're better company."

Skip shook his head. "Well, that's surprisingly gallant coming from a prick who dragged me here to fuck with people he should have ditched years ago. And you totally lucked out, because I am brand-new gay and don't know *shit* about gay issues. For all I know, I voted for the biggest gaycist in Washington."

Carpenter's chuckle was pure evil. "Now *that* would be a discussion worth having."

So they proceeded to have it, quibbling companionably while they watched the two guys in front of them struggle. Two holes later they were in the middle of a similar discussion about Gamergate when Skip laughed—loudly—at Carpenter's suggestion as to what should happen to one of the trolls responsible for hounding the women who had first dared to mention that misogyny was alive and well. At that point one of the men—a real looker, probably in his late thirties, with silvering brown hair and deep laugh lines around dark brown eyes—turned to look at them.

"You two have been really patient—would you like to play through?" His voice sounded a little familiar, but Skip was too embarrassed to try to place him.

"I'm so sorry," he apologized. "We were being loud. We'll just quiet down and leave you alone—our group should be catching up pretty soon."

Carpenter guffawed because the distance between them and their group was increasing with every hole, and Skip smacked him in the arm.

And then the handsome stranger blew his mind.

"Schipperke?"

Oh good Lord. "Uh, the nice guy who sent me the fruit basket?"

He smiled and offered his hand. "Mason Hayes, VP in charge of sales." He blushed. "Thank you for not suing."

Skip smiled, suddenly embarrassed. "Skipper Keith. Thanks for not being a real douche bag. You were really nice when I was sick."

"Suing?" said Mason's golf buddy.

"Oh God," Mason muttered, covering his eyes. "Please don't tell my little brother I hit on you over the phone!"

Skip and Carpenter laughed, like they were supposed to, and they were introduced to Dane Hayes, a younger, slightly goofier version of his upscale older brother.

"My brother the sexually harassing douche bag?" Dane said, laughing dubiously.

"Naw," Skipper said, feeling generous.

127

"Oh yeah," Mason contradicted. "I was nervous, uncomfortable, and I'd just broken up with my boyfriend to relocate to Tesko. Everything that came out of my mouth was all lose, all the time."

"Ouch," Skip said, and a voice behind them caught their attention. "Oh shit. Carpenter, they're catching up."

"Is that your party?" Mason asked, looking at the two of them with amusement.

"Sadly, yes," Carpenter said. "Don't let us keep you."

Dane laughed. "Here, Mace—let them play with us. I'll go, and we can stay away from whoever they're not excited about seeing."

And just like that, Skip was playing with the mysterious gentleman caller, the one Richie had been so jealous of.

Perhaps if Skip hadn't been so gone over Richie, he might have had cause.

Mason and his brother were funny and warm. Dane was still in veterinarian school, and part of the reason Mason had moved to Sacramento from the Bay Area was to be there for his brother while he finished up at UC Davis.

"Our folks are getting older," Mason said before making a truly awful swing. "I suspect they'll be living up in Sun Hills in a couple of years."

"I still can't believe I know someone going through that much schooling," Carpenter said dryly.

Skip waited until Mason's ball wandered into the rough and they all sighed before he said, "What do you mean? All your friends back there were getting their MBAs and law degrees."

Carpenter grunted before making his own—expertly executed—swing. He *didn't* wait for his ball to bounce a few feet from the hole before saying, "Yeah, but Dane's degree is in something real."

Dane grinned at him, his front teeth slightly askew, and Carpenter happily beamed back.

"Oh my God," Mason said with feeling. "Can you two possibly fall in love when we're done with this hole?"

Skipper laughed and Carpenter blushed. "Sorry," he muttered. "I'm not actually gay, but I'm just so relieved not to have to play with my high school people."

Mason groaned. "God, yes. There are *so* many people from high school I will be happy to never talk to again. What about you, Skipper?"

Skip grunted. "Nobody would remember me," he said, suddenly wishing for Richie. "Everybody back away, let's see if my luck holds."

It did, and they continued to play.

They were at the second-to-last hole when Mason brought Skipper abruptly out of the cloud of unexpected camaraderie.

"Wait a minute, Skip—if Carpenter's not gay, who's your boyfriend? Didn't you say something about hooking up over the weekends?"

Skip had been just about to set up for his swing, and he suddenly deflated and cast an unhappy look over his shoulder. "He, uh, had sort of a family emergency." Skip had checked his phone surreptitiously a few times, and Richie hadn't been able to respond. Skip figured that if he didn't get a text responding to *Played golf with Gentleman Caller*, then Richie was either busting his hump or had busted his phone.

"You didn't go help?" Mason asked, surprised.

"It's complicated," Carpenter said for him. "Go ahead and swing, Skip. You might win your first round of golf, and I don't want to jinx it."

Skip grinned appreciatively, cleared his mind, and swung.

It was funny, how golf and soccer were such different sports, but there was still that connecting moment, when the club hit the ball right in the sweet spot, or when the foot hit the much bigger ball, and you knew when it was going to be good.

Skipper watched the ball arch up into the November blue sky before plummeting back down on the green and knew it was good.

BUT THE brief reprieve didn't stop the story from spilling out as Skip proceeded to birdie. He did win, at three under par for the course, and

Carpenter assured him he was some sort of prodigy while at the same time Mason tried to wiggle more of the story out of both of them.

"So... Richie," Mason said for the fifth time as they were walking to the club. "He didn't *want* your help?"

Skip grunted. "His dad would probably beat the shit out of me if I showed up there now."

Mason put his hand on Skip's shoulder then, and Skip paused while Dane and Carpenter continued into the club. "Skip, do you *want* to help him?"

Skip frowned unhappily. That hand on his shoulder felt *really* good, and Mason had been warm and kind and funny and... well... *gay*. Not in the obvious television way, but in the "I'd totally want you if you weren't taken" way.

He just wasn't sure if this was a come-on or not.

"Yeah," Skip said, stepping smoothly backward. "I really want to help him. I *hate* that I won't see him until after Thanksgiving. I...." *I'm afraid he's going to try so hard to forget about us that he succeeds.* "I'm used to seeing him more," he finished weakly.

Mason sighed and looked at him wistfully from earth brown eyes. "Skip, I don't want to... you know... intrude, but...." He laughed and dragged a hand through *very* well cut hair. "Look, I hit on you *before* I saw you. You're... you know. Not bad on the eyes. Just...."

Skip found he was blushing, shifting from foot to foot and uncomfortable in a way that he'd never been with Richie. But his stomach also ached a little from holding it in, which meant Skip wanted this guy to find him attractive too.

"I...." Oh Lord. Men did not say what he was about to say in front of each other. "I really love him. If this doesn't work out, I'm going to be broken for a long time."

Mason shrugged, but he didn't, thank God, look hurt. "And *that's* why you're turning my key, Skipper. Because you'd say that about him without reservation. I'll just have to look for someone I *don't* work with for me!"

Skip blushed. "Well, you know. Think before you talk, and I'm sure it will happen."

Mason had a sweet laugh, but it wasn't manic. He didn't tilt his head back and bounce on his toes. By the time Carpenter's friends dragged their sorry asses into the club and got introduced to Mason and Dane, Skipper had stopped sucking his stomach in at all—and he must have checked his phone about six thousand times.

CARPENTER GOT him home about four in the afternoon, and the first thing he did was mow the lawn and rake before the last of the light failed, and the rain came about a half an hour after that. He spent the evening eating a can of soup and paying bills, and he was falling asleep on the couch watching a really stupid movie on television around ten o'clock. When he asked himself why it was so goddamned important that he finish watching *Route 666*, he realized he was checking his phone every time he jerked himself awake.

Hell.

He had just crawled into bed when he heard a knock on the door. Richie was standing under the porch, his orange hair speckled with rain.

Skip hauled him inside and into his arms without a word.

Ah, Richie… he must have eaten a box of Tic Tacs, because he tasted like mints with a nicotine chaser, but Skip didn't care. Skip had him backed up against the door and was holding him in place while he ravaged his mouth, hard and possessive and needy, and Richie returned in kind. Richie's clothes tumbled to the floor, and Skip stepped away to let him kick off his shoes. Richie took the space and ran with it, backing Skip onto the couch until he fell sprawling on it and then kissed Skip while they ground against each other.

Skip's hands shook in his hair, and his hips thrust upward spasmodically, needing… needing… needing so damned hard.

Richie pulled away for a moment and searched Skip's eyes. "He hit on you?" he asked.

Skip shook his head. "He wanted to. I told him I was taken."

Richie nodded, and his eyes got wide and shiny. "You *are* taken," he muttered. "You're *mine*."

He slid off of Skip then and took the two steps across the room for his pants so he could pull lube out of the pocket. Skip got up too, so when Richie tried to bend over, ass up, Skip could yank on his hair and say, "On your back, Richie. Face me."

Richie stretched out lengthwise on the couch, and lifted his legs, hugging them to his chest. Skip's whole body quivered—they'd done this enough that his cock didn't need any pointers for where to go, it just needed *in*.

Still, he remembered his manners, remembered to stretch, to ask permission, and Richie's harsh breathing and half-whimpered begging filled his ears.

"You like this?" Skip asked, two fingers sheathed and scissoring inside Richie's body. "You think this is awesome?"

"Yeah," Richie breathed. "C'mon, Skip… want!"

"All you gotta do is *be* here!" Skip snapped, and then he mounted his lover's scrawny, fighting body and drove inside.

Richie let out a moan and wrapped his legs around Skipper's hips and screamed, "Fucking *hard*!"

Skip fucked him so hard he couldn't make any more words. Fucked him so hard and so fast he couldn't even beg. Skip's hips got numb from banging against Richie's bony ass, and Richie sobbed for breath but he didn't ask for it harder because Skip loved him just as hard as he could.

Richie's shriek of orgasm probably echoed down the street, but Skip didn't care. Richie shot without touching himself, the come spattering across Skip's chest, even under his chin, and Richie let out breathless little moans with every thrust after that.

"Please," he managed, no wind left. "Please, Skipper…."

The begging broke Skip, tore his climax right out of him, his entire body exploding into white light before he could even cry out.

He came to with his face buried in the hollow of Richie's neck, trying hard not to laugh and cry.

"Skip," Richie whispered. "Skipper, I've got to go."

Skip pushed up on his elbows and thought about getting mad. "You've got to do *what*?" he asked in disbelief. His arms tightened around Richie's shoulders, and for a moment, Richie didn't fight him.

"I told my dad I was going out for beer," Richie said apologetically. "I told you—he's been checking for me at night—"

"Richie!" Skip buried his face back in the hollow of Richie's neck and then said the obvious. "You're twenty-five years old!"

Richie laughed helplessly. "Yeah," he said, nuzzling Skip's ear. He had quite a bit of stubble—had probably gone without shaving for a week. "Took me that long to figure out what I want, and apparently I'm not supposed to have it."

"I don't see why not," Skip muttered, feeling sulky. "Seriously, why the crackdown?" Richie made an uncomfortable sound and Skip pushed up. "Am I crushing you?"

"Don't you dare move," Richie said huskily. "No. It's... so, you know how I told you that the vandalism ended up being a lot of useless junk?"

"Yeah," Skip said. That was easy to remember because a deep and terrible suspicion had started in his stomach at the time. "You said you thought most of the valuable stuff had been taken already."

Richie nodded and then looked so lonely Skip wanted to cry. "Well, Dad didn't listen to me the first couple of times I said it, but then the insurance people came out and started looking around."

"And?"

Richie closed those infinity-pool green eyes and almost melted into the couch beneath him. "And they agreed with me. Someone had been taking shit for a month, and the vandalism was to cover it up."

Skip didn't say anything for a moment. He knew where this was going, but he was pretty sure Richie needed to say it anyway. "The alarms were disabled."

"Yeah," Richie said.

"What do they say?"

Richie's eyes opened, and they were shiny and red rimmed. "See, the insurance people came by, and they had officers with them, and they asked to talk to Paul and Rob, and... and nothing. Dad couldn't get them on the phone, Kay couldn't get them on the phone—and then Kay ran into their room in the house and their stuff was all gone."

"Oh no...."

133

"So the cops searched the place, and then they searched *my* place, which was *hilarious* because I don't have anything—they actually asked me how much I paid for rent. I swear to God, a cop turned to my father and told him he was robbing his own son blind." Richie's lip curled up slightly. "That was sort of awesome, actually."

Skip's lip curled in an entirely different way. "Swell," he muttered. "So you're going back why?"

"Because...." Richie's voice sank thoughtfully, which was good—it meant he was really giving some attention to the idea. "I don't know," he said at last, and Skip's heart lightened. "He's just... you know. My dad. My mom left him and all he had was me. For a few years, it was just... you know, us. I mean, he's got a flaky sister, but I cooked the dinner and cleaned the house, and we were a family." His voice cracked for a moment. "Some of that went away with Kay, but I don't... he hasn't been a monster, you know? Don't you owe it to family?"

"I wouldn't know," Skip said weakly. He had nothing. "I just don't want you to go."

Richie reached up and stroked his cheek. "Hardly any stubble," he said with a small smile. "Did he really hit on you?"

Skip captured his hand, turned, and kissed his palm. "No. He said he was interested. But he got it. He's a friend."

Richie nodded. "Okay. I'll set the alarm and leave real early." He arched up and kissed the corner of Skip's mouth. "If this guy's stupid enough to let you go, I should be smart enough to stay for a while."

Skip kissed him for real, and like they tended to do, this kiss went on for a while. When he was done, Richie was half-asleep and still kissing. Skip laughed a little and reluctantly got off the couch. He helped Richie up, and the two of them walked, naked, toward the bedroom. Richie stopped in midmarch and started gathering his clothes, pulling his phone from his pocket as he did so.

"No texts," he said with some gratification. "Dad fell asleep. He'll wake up at six—if I'm up at four, I won't have to deal with his bullshit."

"That's a shitty time to get up," Skip mumbled. God—four in the morning?

"Maybe five," Richie conceded with a grunt. He moved in front of Skip, and just the heat from his silhouette radiated comfort.

"Are you still putting the place right?"

"We've got about four, five more days' work to go," Richie confirmed. "Dad says we'll work through Thanksgiving and do the family thing Friday."

Skipper let a sound of protest escape, and Richie looked behind him, grabbing his hand. "Yeah, I know. No long practice on Friday. I know we were going to… you know. Come out, do the whole thing with the team together, but not this week." He sighed. "I'm so sorry, man."

"It's all right," Skip muttered, stowing the hurt away. Friday's practice was sort of special even *without* their grand plan to talk to the team, but his eyes were on the long game now. "It'll be worth it if you can get away during the weekend."

Richie stopped in the doorway and turned into a full-body, naked hug. "Being with you is worth anything," he said simply. "Let me get my dad settled. Let me feel like I'm not deserting him. And then it'll be you and me, okay?"

"Yeah, okay," Skip mumbled into his hair. "Yeah." *Anything, just stay with me tonight. Just sleep in my bed, be there in the morning.*

He didn't say it out loud, but they slid into bed. Skip was the big spoon, and he didn't let go all night.

RICHIE'S PHONE buzzed at ass-crack-thirty, and Skip got out of bed with him to make coffee while he was in the shower. Richie's car was more than comfortably ruffled when Skip went out to get Richie's travel coffee mug—it was full of fast-food wrappers and even had some butts in the ashtrays. But Skip didn't say a word, just had Richie's coffee ready, lots of cream and sugar, by the time Richie was dressed.

Richie took the mug from Skip's hands and smiled gamely at him. "You trying to spoil me into staying?" he asked playfully.

"Will it work?"

Richie took a sip and winked. "It might."

Skip went in for a kiss, and Richie gave him a brief one but then pulled back. "No killer kisses, 'kay, Skipper? I've got to go clean up my family shit. Can't do it all day if I'm thinking about your kiss."

Skip kissed his temple instead. "Love you, Richie."

"Love you back."

Then he was gone.

Castles in the Sky

"You look like shit," Carpenter said to him that morning. "What happened?"

Skipper groaned, scrubbing his face with his hands. "Richie stopped by last night."

"Do you feel used?" Carpenter asked, horrified, and Skip had to laugh.

"Yeah, sort of, but in a good way. No, his life just got crazy complicated. The chimp brothers actually ripped off the family, his dad is getting more psychotic by the nanosecond—but you know what?"

"What?"

"He left that all behind for me. He'll do it again."

Carpenter let out a breath. "Yeah. Sure, Skip."

Skip could tell he wanted to say more, but at that moment Skip's phone rang. Mason was on the other end, asking in a kind and professional manner if Skip could help him with his browser. Skip had a job to do that he didn't hate, and a little bit of hope. It would do.

The hope sustained him for the rest of the week. On Wednesday night he baked seven loaves of basic bread, and called up Galvan, Jefferson, and Owens and asked them if they wanted some. He brought two over to Carpenter's parents' place and kept two for him and Richie, wrapped tight in tinfoil after the initial cooling period. He'd had a couple of pieces of one of the loaves, and it had turned out yeasty and comforting, which as far as he was concerned was all bread *should* be.

Carpenter's parents lived up in the foothills, in one of the developments back by Auburn/Folsom Road. The houses there were *amazing*, and since Skip and Carpenter were driving up from Carmichael together, Skip got several chances to tell Carpenter how much he sucked because of it.

"Seriously? 'Just come up to my parents' place, Skip, it's got like seventeen rooms—'"

"Fifteen," Carpenter said uncomfortably.

"And maid's quarters—"

"She doesn't stay overnight!"

"And a ginormous fucking garage for our three different Rolls-Royces!" Skip finished viciously as—at Carpenter's direction—they pulled into one of the larger houses in the rather fantastic development. "Holy fuck, Carpenter—that brick house has *turrets*. This is fucking Granite Bay and that house has *turrets*. And maid's quarters, I don't *care* if she goes home to her family. You couldn't have *warned* me about this?"

"What's to warn—"

"You can fit my house in your family room!" Skip gestured to the grand monstrosity in front of them. "I could have at *least* worn a tie!"

Carpenter grunted. "You can't make a big deal out of the money," he said, sounding like it was a rule.

"Carpenter—"

"And you have to call me Clay. My parents think we're friends."

"We *are* friends," Skip said. "You took me golfing. I think that makes us brothers." He pulled his teeny tiny car to a stop behind five other cars—Lexus being the *least* premium among them—and dragged his hands through his hair. He'd gotten his hair cut on Saturday, and he and Richie had been so… otherwise involved that he hadn't had a chance to ask Richie if he liked it. About four years earlier, Skip had gotten a Bieber, and Richie had been the first person to come right out and say it looked like crap and for fuck's sake go get a real haircut like a man. Hearing that it looked good from Richie would have meant something.

"Well if we're friends, the money shouldn't matter!" Carpenter said triumphantly, pulling Skip out of *that* line of thinking. "This is a perfectly normal house in a perfectly normal suburb!" He was balancing a big dish of something on his lap, or Skip was pretty sure he would have been gesticulating madly to try to convince Skip that the boogie man did not live in a big house in Granite Bay.

"We *are* friends," Skip said bitterly, "but dude." He looked at this big house with the nice yard and the cars. "Dude." He should have known—seriously, he should have known. Carpenter's dad had a tee time at the Fair Oaks golf range the weekend before Thanksgiving— Skip totally should have known. But he hadn't, and the extent of the… the *opulence* shocked him. His phone buzzed in his pocket, and he read Richie's message, grateful for the distraction before he started to hyperventilate.

We're finally fucking done. Happy Thanksgiving to me, I can go to sleep now.

Oh God. Richie had been texting him at nine o'clock at night for the past three nights. The night before, while Skip had been waiting for the last batch of bread to bake, he'd gotten a string of pictures, from the morning when Richie first walked in and saw that the lot had been vandalized to the day before, when it had been cleaned and rearranged and made—hopefully—ready to start up business on Monday.

There wouldn't be much business. There *couldn't* be. There was quite simply not that much left.

Seeing those pictures, Skip had gotten a bigger picture of Richie's reasons for staying close to his father. Richie had been the one by his dad's side, cleaning up the business that his dad had built from a few used cars in his driveway. Richie had been the one who had drawn up the insurance papers and entered everything into the computer. The tech school training that his dad and Kay had constantly given him shit about was going to allow his dad to keep buying inventory and to hopefully reopen on the Monday after Thanksgiving. Maybe.

Richie felt *needed*, and Skip couldn't hold that against him. And looking at those pictures, he hadn't been able to argue with Richie leaving his bed to go back out and help. Hell, when Skip had Wednesday off—even without seeing the pictures—he'd texted that he was coming over to help. He'd nearly gotten there before Richie *called*—catching him while he was stopped at the McDonald's drive-through for coffee—and begged him not to do it.

"Please, Skip. Dad's just… he's not rational right now, okay? I don't know how Paul and Rob being douche bags came down to being your fault, but after Sunday night, I can't take a leak without him blaming you for making me have to pee."

"Does he know you left?"

"Yeah, he figured it out Monday night when he asked me if I had any beer."

"Ugh… yeah—sort of needed to cover your tracks."

"I'm saying. But don't come and help, okay? I mean, I know you mean well, but he's just going to yell at you and say ugly shit—"

"Has he been saying ugly shit to you?" Oh God! Richie!

"Yeah. Yeah, Skip, he has. But don't worry about it. We should be done Thanksgiving, and we're having dinner Friday. He's not going to get ugly if all his and Kay's family are over—especially not when Rob and Paul are in the fucking wind. Just hang in there, Skipper. I know you just want to help me, but if you can wait until Saturday, and the game, I should be able to come see you, okay? After that, you and I can get a little back to normal."

That had been yesterday morning. Today, Thanksgiving, when Skip finally had something to be thankful for, he was stuck staring at the ginormous castle Carpenter had hauled him to and wondering what he'd ever imagined as normal.

He picked up the phone and texted, *I miss you so fucking bad. I should be there with you.*

"This is normal?" he asked Carpenter weakly when he was done.

"How's Richie?" Carpenter asked gently.

"He gets to sleep on Thanksgiving, and I apparently still don't get to come on the property."

Carpenter sighed. "C'mon, Skipper. Let's go inside and you can meet my folks and my aunt and uncle. They'll question you about your childhood and try to feed you tofurkey, and afterwards we can go to your place and eat hamburgers and play video games."

Skip looked at him mournfully, thinking that was probably what he'd be doing with Richie if Rob and Paul hadn't been horrible people.

And if Richie's dad hadn't decided that no amount of mentholyptus could cover the smell of sex.

"Yeah, okay," Skip said, resignation washing over him. He wasn't going to see Richie tomorrow. Richie was going to have *his* Thanksgiving tomorrow, and Skip wasn't invited.

Skip wanted to cry.

"C'mon," Carpenter said gently.

Skip swallowed and smiled gamely at him, letting his misery show for maybe the first time since Richie had texted last Friday. They'd played—and lost—without Richie that Saturday, and Skip had bailed on the pizza and beer, claiming exhaustion. He hadn't been able to tell everyone he just couldn't socialize, couldn't laugh and smile, not when he knew Richie was working his ass off and Skip didn't get to help.

This was stupid, he told himself resolutely. Richie wasn't *dead*. He wasn't *deployed* or in another country. But nothing worked, because the point, Skipper was beginning to realize, was that he wasn't *there*.

Skip needed him *there*.

"Yeah," Skip heard himself saying from far away. "Yeah. Okay. Let's go be family."

CARPENTER'S MOTHER and father were tanned, attractive, fit people, and at first Skip sort of expected to hate them on sight. A part of him was pretty sure their tanned, attractive fitness had come at Carpenter's expense.

But you didn't just greet a couple of people inviting you into their home with "Hi, Mr. and Mrs. Carpenter, so how *did* you make your son fat?"

Instead he said "Hi!" and handed them two loaves of bread, still warm from the oven he'd pulled them out of that morning.

Mrs. Carpenter—Cheryl—was delighted.

"Oh, how lovely! You made this?"

Skip nodded, taking kudos for the world's easiest bread recipe. It had been something his mom had taught him before the divorce, and he'd managed to hold on to it into adulthood. "Yes, ma'am. It's one of maybe five things I can cook."

"So is it leavened or unleavened?"

"Uh, it's got yeast—"

"What kind of flour did you use?"

"Uh, the multipurpose kind, you know—"

"So not gluten-free?" she asked, looking disappointed. She was one of those fiftyish women who looked late thirtyish if you didn't count the deepness of the smile grooves by her eyes. Her hair was frosted and held up at her nape with a clip. Skip thought wistfully that she looked like the kind of mom any boy would want as an adult.

"No, ma'am, I'm sorry. Carp, er, Clay didn't tell me if you had any allergies."

"No, no," she said, smiling bravely as though they'd all get through it. "It's just that wheat flour is so bad for you. But that's okay. It's Thanksgiving and we're having vegan cheese in with the mashed cauli-tatoes and salty gravy on the tofurkey—we can afford one more indulgence."

Skip smiled at her, feeling like he'd just gotten a pat on the head for a macaroni necklace, and Cheryl Carpenter disappeared into the kitchen.

"I should have brought wine," Skip said in an undertone.

"If it's less than two hundred dollars a bottle, they use it in the gravy," Clay said, and Skip shot him a killing look. "I'm serious!" Clay maintained, hands up. Then he cast a determined smile over Skip's shoulder. "Hi, Dad!"

"Clay!" Skip moved so Clyde Carpenter could come embrace his son.

Yeah, a little awkward, and when the vegetable plates came out, Skip heeded Clay's frantically waved hands and stayed the hell away from the dip. But Clay's parents were friendly, and *very* liberal, and they were as supportive as possible of their slacking, video-game-playing son, even when he was overshadowed by his rather spectacular sister.

Skip sat on the cushioned stone of the fireplace apron in a room with a plush berber carpet and cream-colored walls that were pristine and flawlessly painted. He sipped really expensive wine and noshed on stuff he'd never heard of while listening to two people sincerely intertwine the adventures of their flawless perfect daughter with the more modest accomplishments of their son.

"Sabrina is doing really well at Stanford," Clyde said as Skipper tried to forget he'd just eaten bean curd and sprouts. "She's earned another grant, Clay. She was sorry she didn't make it up, but they've taken the twins to help volunteer at a child cancer ward for Thanksgiving."

"I miss them," Clay said, and although his voice, too, rang with sincerity, Skip was pretty sure he detected some understandable relief.

"Of course—and you met with Austen, right?"

"Yeah, but Skip and I were sort of ahead of the group during golf. I didn't get a chance to talk."

Skip looked at Carpenter quizzically and he shrugged. "Austen's my sister's brother-in-law," he said weakly.

Skip stared at him, because they'd *both* blown the guy off for a prick, and if Skip had known he was family, he probably would have made more of an effort.

Carpenter smiled innocently back and then said to his family, "I, uh, joined Skipper's soccer team." As a diversion, it worked perfectly.

"Clay!" his mother said delightedly. "You didn't tell us that! Skipper—how's he doing?"

"He's doing great," Skip said with enthusiasm.

"Well, he never was very fast," Clay's uncle Carter said with a pitying look. "He couldn't make it in any of his high school teams."

"Yeah, well, high school coaches don't have any patience," Skip said staunchly. "He sort of got thrown into the deep end, really. At first we just needed him to sub for the defense, and he did a real good job there—smart player, listens, thinks on the field. But after the first game, I got sick, and the next game Richie—uhm, er, our,

143

uh, forward"—he charged on through the blush—"couldn't play last week, and he played both games like a champ. Last week it was like he'd been there for years."

"That's wonderful, Clay!" his father said, beaming. "I always knew you could enjoy sports—sometimes it just needs to happen at the right time, you know?"

"So what made this the right time?" Uncle Carter said, narrowing his eyes.

Skip and Clay exchanged glances, and Clay shrugged and held out his hand. "You were doing fine," he said, smiling.

"Well, mostly he was just fun to talk to, and Richie liked him, so it was great to have him on the team."

"Is Richie cocaptain?" Carter asked, all curiosity. Uncle Carter had a wife, Candace, who was playing games with their children in the adjoining room, and Skip wished he'd wandered in there.

"Uh, no," Skip said and then decided to go for broke. "Richie's my boyfriend. His opinion's sort of important."

"Oh!" Carter said, laughing—but not unkindly. "You're right. His opinion counts. Why isn't he here today?"

"Uh." Skip pulled at his collar. "Someone sort of broke into his family business last week and vandalized it. Did a really good job of it. He just texted me and said he barely finished cleanup. He's crashing at his place, and tomorrow his family is having their Thanksgiving."

"So you get two meals, then?"

Oh God. Shoot him now. "No, sir, only one."

"Oh," Carter said, and he sounded… compassionate. Like he understood.

"That is a shame," Clay's father added, and again, that compassionate smile.

Suddenly Skipper got it, about family being a curse and a blessing at the same time. Yeah, he'd probably have food issues too if he grew up in this house—but he could see why Carpenter would want to bring a friend here, especially one who had no family and needed people.

But that didn't mean that after a Unitarian prayer (apparently Aunt Candace was a youth pastor because… well, because these people!), when the tofurkey and cauliflower/vegan cheese mash was passed around, Skipper didn't eat more than his share of bread.

Carpenter met his eyes over a bite of tofurkey with pained gratitude, and Skipper nodded.

Oh yeah. They were so stopping for a burger and fries on the way home.

CARPENTER CRASHED on his couch that night, after they polished off the burgers, the fries, and half of the cherry pie and ice cream Skipper had gone into Safeway for before they got home.

Yeah, part of it was because tofurkey was maybe not going into his top-ten lists of ways to stay healthy, no matter how much he wanted to go from a four-pack down to six.

The other part was that Skipper felt the bone-deep need for a carbohydrate pity party that he didn't even want to reveal to Carpenter. But Carpenter knew. If nothing else, Carpenter had his own need for carbs.

"She's brilliant," Carpenter said through a mouthful of pie. "My sister, she's brilliant. She always was. I'd be struggling with my algebra in the seventh grade and she'd be like, 'Oh, Clay, it's just this and then this and then this and then you pull an integer out your ear and shit out the answer!' But she was always so *nice* about it. And I wanted to be a big hateful, envious turd, but how can you be when she's such a sweetheart? I mean… she took her twins to a *cancer ward* on Thanksgiving so they knew how to be thankful. Even her husband—I mean, he *could* be a prick like Austen, but no. He's like Austen's polar opposite—warm, kind, real. He raises money for medical care for underprivileged youth. How do you… how do you compete with that?"

Skip gave him another dollop of vanilla. "You stay at a friend's house when he's sick and make sure he has someplace to go during what could be the loneliest holiday of the year," he said. "And you make

145

your *friend* remember what it's like to be thankful on Thanksgiving. Good karma *done*, Carpenter. Check it off the list. Enjoy your pie."

"I will, brother—but I'm going to cut you off. I know you, and you will *hate* yourself in the morning."

Skip looked at the last half of the piece on his plate miserably and took a resolute bite. Nope. Didn't help. "He... I mean, I texted him pictures of the house and stuff, and you know, had your family pose. Sent him that."

"Nothing back?" Carpenter asked, his voice quiet.

Skip shook his head and put his palms to his eyes to stop the stupid burning. "I... maybe he changed his mind," he said quietly, and then, last Sunday forgotten, he said what was really in his heart. "Maybe he decided he didn't want to follow me to gay league after all."

"Maybe he just needs an engraved invitation," Carpenter said practically. "I mean, Skip, not everybody can just walk on a soccer field and take charge. Some of us need a little direction, you know?"

Skip stared at him.

"What?"

"It's... it's *rec league soccer!*" he flailed, like that explained everything. "I'm not... I mean... the name thing that everyone's so rock solid about? That started as a *joke*. We recruited a coach, but he got a better offer from a comp league team, and there we were, our first game, and everybody's going, 'Who's playing where? What do we do now?' And I knew me, Richie, and McAlister were our best strikers and Menendez, Jimenez, Thomas, and Galvan were our best defenders, and Owens and Jefferson and Cooper could run for years, and Singh got goalie by default, you know? And I told Richie he was center and he turned around and saluted and said, 'Aye-aye, Skipper!' And that was it. Everybody just *called me this stupid name*! And I don't mind the name, really—but... but it was like everybody forgot that I was just making it up as I went along!"

Skip was standing up by this time, gesticulating madly, his voice pitching with hurt.

146

And abruptly he sat down again, the chair creaking ominously beneath his ass.

"Like everyone assumes I know what to do just because my name is Skipper. But I need Richie to captain this fuckin' ship, Clay. I...."

He closed his eyes. When he'd been a kid, his mom had been drunk in her room and school had been insufferable. His pants had been ripping in the ass, and he had no friends. He'd lie down in his room and close his eyes and plan what he'd do when he passed his next test and ran his next mile and graduated from this shitty high school and got a job that would pay a mortgage, and had a house and a pet and friends and a girlfriend (at the time) of his own. He imagined *past* the pain to a time when things didn't hurt anymore, and he tried to do that now.

How would he captain this fuckin' ship without Richie? What if Richie just dropped out of his life entirely, leaving Skipper gay and alone and starting his personal life from scratch?

And the pain didn't go away.

He dropped his head into his arms and tried hard not to cry. Mostly he succeeded. Clay finished off Skip's pie for him and waited until he stood up and proposed *Witch Hunter 4*. Skip was finally getting good at that one.

HE WENT to bed around twelve, after checking his phone about six million times for a message. Finally, right before he dropped off to sleep, Richie texted.

Jesus, Skipper. It took me half an hour to read through the travelogue.

Skip stared at the text and narrowly avoided punching in "Where the fuck you been????"

I missed you today.

Yeah—I fell asleep and I just woke up now. Dad and Kay are prepping turkey and fighting—I can hear them through the walls.

Why are they fighting?

147

Cause Dad finally asked her if she knows where Paul and Rob are when she told the insurance people she didn't. I think it's occurred to both of them that her sons aren't coming back, and that they took a fuckton of money with them.

That sucks.

I hate them, Richie texted, and Skip could hear his voice, with the words echoing from his stomach. He hit Call.

"I don't blame you," he said when Richie answered.

"God, I needed to hear your voice," Richie said, and he sounded broken and sad and tired.

"You fuckin' think?" Skipper shot at him. "All goddamned day. Now tell me about the yard."

He let Richie talk to him about forklift rentals and insurance assholes and cars that were half-buried in mud. The talk washed over him, Skip going "Uh-huh, yeah, okay" but so glad to be a part of it, so glad Richie needed him there, that he would have listened to it all night if he had to, just so they weren't alone.

Richie rambled to a halt after about half an hour, though, then changed the subject to the family gathering the next day. Skip closed tired eyes as he talked about how awful it was going to be.

"I figure," Richie said, "we can gauge who knew or helped the two of them get away with all of this by who shows up. When Kay's whole family bails, there's gonna be a fight that makes the one they're having now look like fuzzy bunnies humping."

"Oh my God," Skip muttered. "Richie, I know this is… I mean, the cops aren't *my* first line of defense either, but have you thought about… I mean, if the insurance company catches you—"

"I'm not going to fuckin' jail for them," Richie said disgustedly. "Not a damned one of them. Not even my dad. Nope, I'm being absolutely honest, man, above fucking board. We had to talk to the police to put a claim number on the insurance forms, and if one of those guys even thought to ask me if I knew who did it, I'd be singing like a… a… a…."

"Tofurkey?" Skip suggested, just to see if he'd laugh.

148

He did, his giggles echoing against his pillow as he huddled in his bed. Skip had been there a few times, and Richie lived more simply than even Skip. His bed consisted of a mattress on box springs on top of a basic rail frame, backed up in the corner of the bedroom by a window.

Skip remembered that it didn't even have a comforter, just a couple of blankets and some basic white sheets.

No wonder Richie had been so excited about decorating Skip's place for Thanksgiving. He felt like he was making his place…

His place.

Like he was decorating his home.

Richie had wound completely down now, his voice slurred and loopy as he giggled over how Kay kept wailing, "They're my babies and I love them!" loud enough to be heard through the garage.

"Richie?" Skip said, not wanting to drop a bomb on him right now but needing Richie to hear him. "Richie—I just want you to be home."

"Yeah, Skip. Me too. I'll come home Saturday, okay? Won't leave again 'til… M…." And he fell asleep right in the middle of that sentence, leaving Skip thinking that Richie didn't need to move out into his own apartment to have another place to live.

THE SCORPIONS had managed to secure a practice field from three to five the next day, meaning they were starting out in the late afternoon but it would be near full dark by the time they were done.

Skip got there early, of course, with a big cooler full of water and sports drinks and even some dried fruit since it was such a long practice. He had everybody but McAlister there by the time four o'clock rolled around. There'd been another storm the week before, and McAlister worked for a tree service, so it was his busy time—Skip didn't think too much about it.

They were gathered around the cooler for a break when McAlister strode across the field in his waffle-stompers and Day-Glo orange vest, looking fit to kill.

"Mac?" Owens called out. "Where's your gear? Man, you can't play wearing that!"

"I'm not gonna fuckin' play for this team anymore!" McAlister shouted. His face was red with exertion and apparently anger, and he strode down across the field straight to Skipper. "I'm not gonna play for a fuckin' fairy, asshole. You all better get the fuck out of here too, or he'll make you fuckin' gay just like he did to Scoggins!"

Skip had never really felt his jaw drop before. "I'm sorry?"

"Yeah—you think nobody fuckin' saw you after the last practice, but you're *wrong*, faggot. My *dad* saw you, and we started talking over Thanksgiving about where my team practiced, and he told me about two guys going at it, fucking disgusting, a redheaded guy and a blond guy, tongues down each other's throats and everything. I heard your voice on the line this morning reminding us about practice and I about *puked*."

He really hammered the word "puked," complete with spittle, and Skipper shivered under the chilly November sun, looking back at the faces of the team he'd assembled through goodwill and good sportsmanship alone.

"So is it true?" Jefferson asked into the silence. "You and Scoggins hooking up?"

Skip swallowed and wished for Richie so hard he was surprised he didn't hear Richie's voice in his head. "Yeah," he said quietly. "Since right before Halloween. We're...." Oh please, Richie, let this be true. "I'm hoping he'll move in with me soon."

"Good for you!" Jefferson clapped his back hard enough to tingle.

"Yeah, man—good for you!" The chorus of well wishes made his knees weak, and he gave a watery smile to his team surrounding him on the field.

"Hey!" Owens said, and for a moment Skip's heart stalled. Oh God, no, let this not be the other shoe. "Is this why Scoggins didn't call us in to take care of you when you were sick? Was he afraid you'd say something?"

"Oh my God!" Carpenter shook his head. "Did you guys know he fucking *babbles* when he's sick!"

"Well, uh, yeah," Menendez said. "That's how we knew Skip sort of crushed on Richie in the first place."

"I did *not* know that," Jimenez said, shrugging. "But that's okay, because my little brother is gay, and I just can't hate, you know?"

"Oh God," Skip moaned good-naturedly. "Really? You all knew? 'Cause it took the two of us by surprise!"

Catcalls and hollers met that announcement, Thomas and Cooper joining in, and for a moment, riding the glow of good wishes, Skip forgot McAlister and his concentrated venom, even though the big Irishman was standing right in front of him.

"So that's it?" Mac interrupted, obviously floundering. "You guys find out our captain's a fag and you just… just congratulate him?"

"That's not a very nice word," Singh said, his diction precise. "What's the matter, McAlister—does it offend your manhood that a gay man is a better player than you?"

"What *offends* me," McAlister snarled, his face contorted and ugly in a way that Skip found truly frightening, "is that this cocksucker and his little butt-buddy have run this team into the ground like it's some sort of blow job buffet! Jesus, Keith, your little *boy*friend can't play for shit, and you just keep putting him on the front line like he can blow us into first place again!"

They had to pull Skipper off of him.

One moment he was standing there, letting all of that irrational hatred roll off his back, and seriously wondering when rec league soccer, a sport made up of guys playing after work to let off steam, became a contender for more than a round of beers after the game.

The next minute McAlister was on the ground hitting Skip's fists with his face and the entire team was hauling Skip off and telling him that it wasn't fucking worth it. Carpenter and Owens each held one of Skip's arms as Jefferson and Menendez pulled McAlister out of the mud.

"He beat you fair and square," Thomas said over their shoulders. He was a tall guy, all elbows, and he sounded like a schoolteacher

151

should as he lectured. "You tell the police, and we all tell them that you let a gay man pound your nose until it broke."

Cooper—their shortest player besides Richie—stepped forward and stood in his face. "We're done here, Mac," he said seriously. "The rest of the team doesn't give a shit—and you've said too goddamned much. If you ever want to play with *us* again, we're going to need a big fucking apology. Otherwise you need to get the fuck off our field."

Skip watched him slump forward suddenly, like it had never occurred to him that he could lose his team, lose his friends, his peer group, his recreation after work, by buying into the same prejudice his father did. For a moment Skip felt sorry for him—Skip had *known* what was at risk. He'd been ready to lose all his people.

McAlister had never thought that would happen to him.

"Really?" he asked, sounding puzzled and lost. "Seriously? You're going to pick a f—"

"You say the F-word again and we will fucking hurt you," Jimenez snarled, and unlike Menendez, Jimenez actually knew what it was like to live in the not-wonderful part of town. He'd had to fight for his law degree.

"The world has fucking changed," McAlister muttered. "And not for the better."

He turned around and stalked off the field, leaving the team breathing hard with adrenaline and excitement.

"Oh holy fucking wow," Skipper said into the sudden quiet. "You guys—I mean, I sort of hoped you wouldn't all hate me, but I just never expected that."

"Well yeah, Skipper," Galvan and Owens said in tandem. Then Owens continued, although usually he let Galvan do the talking. "I mean, six years we've had each other's backs. We're not going to let that go because *that* asshole suddenly buys a clue. You're, you know. You and Scoggins are our friends."

Skip grinned shyly back, and then Thomas snagged a practice ball and started showboating, and Menendez had him pass it over. Carpenter gave Skipper a couple of clean towels so he could wrap his knuckles—and wipe the blood off his cheek, since McAlister had gotten his own blows in—and by the time Skipper had cleaned up, the guys were heavily invested in a game of Hot Potato, the kind where everybody got to play and the only rule was don't drop the fucking ball.

For the last half hour as the light died and winter took over their little corner of the world, Skipper got to play with his team. When he'd been a little kid hiding in his room, dreaming of a better future and friends, this moment here, friends calling his name and laughing and cheering him on, *this* moment was the one he'd been dreaming of.

When it was over and everybody had moved to their cars, volunteers helping with the snack table and the ice chest, Skipper stood by his car and looked out over the field as the lights clicked on and the next team started.

Carpenter stood at his elbow, ready to hop in his own car and—his words—go soak in a hot bath and dream of girls with nice pert breasts. "Whatcha thinkin', Skip?"

Skip turned to him and smiled a little. "I'm thinking this was a really awesome day. I'm going to go share it with Richie."

Carpenter grinned. "That's my boy."

Skip didn't even go home to change.

A Gateway Drug to Christmas

THE WORLD was full dark by the time Skip turned left on Grant Line. He was very careful not to make the left-hand turn into the scrap yard, and instead drove another half a mile and turned down the long driveway to the house.

In the summer the house was a green oasis of a copse of trees—watered, of course—and a lawn, all in the middle of long grasses that were usually mown as hay. This time of year, if there'd been any rain at all, the hay was still long green grass over star thistle skeletons. The house itself—yellow, two stories, with the little apartment over the garage—was set at an off angle from the road. Anyone coming in could park in a little dirt-and-gravel area by the trees and then circle around to the front walk, which looked south at a ninety-degree angle from the east/west running road. Skip had no idea why anyone would design a house like this—unless it was to be able to ignore the traffic and the vast expanse of nothing that this area still was—but as he parked by the trees, he realized the design had its uses.

Nobody watched him drive up. Nobody watched him park his car right behind Richie's, one of maybe seven cars in the full little parking area. Skip was a secret, a surprise, and if he was lucky, he could see Richie before anybody else saw him.

As he walked around the copse, staying to the shadows, he smelled tobacco and heard a voice swear "Gross!" on the exhale.

Oh God. Skip really *was* the luckiest man on the planet.

"That shit's really bad for you," he said, rounding the corner. Richie was leaning against a tree, glaring at the house and smoking. He was dressed nicely in jeans and a sweater, but the jeans slid around a waist that was a bit stringier than it had been, even since Sunday, and his face was sawtooth lean. He'd shaved recently, but in the light

154

from the porch, Skip could see he'd missed patches. Well, he didn't have anyone to look nice for, maybe.

He saw Skip and he dropped the butt onto the wet earth at the tree's roots and ground it out, his face lighting up in excitement.

"Skip! Oh my God! Holy shit! What are you doing...." His expression fell and he slowed his gallop into what should have been Skip's arms. "Skip, you have to go home, man, my dad cannot *catch* you here—"

"Come home with me."

Richie stopped talking and stared at him. Skip took that last step into Richie's space. He smelled more heavily of tobacco than he ever had, and Skip reckoned part of his reluctance to come by was that Skip would realize how much he'd been smoking lately.

Who cared? Skip would take him, nicotine and all.

Skip looked down and seized his battered, yellowing fingers in his own.

"Skip?" Richie said, uncertain, and Skip caught his eyes and smiled tentatively.

"We... we were outed to the team today. I mean, you weren't there, but McAlister's dad saw us, I guess, and Mac showed up all ready to be a jerk and a bully and...."

Richie's shaking hand found the cut at Skip's cheekbone. "I'll fucking kill him," he said, voice crumbling.

Skip caught the hand near his cheek and held it there. "You don't have to." He smiled, the memory still sweet. "The whole team just sort of shut him down. Told him to get the fuck out of there, they didn't need him if he was going to be an asshole."

"They did what?" Oh, his disbelief was precious. It was, very nearly, Skipper's own.

"They chose us, Richie. They would rather play with us, out and proud, than line up behind McAlister, a big asshole, any day. They *chose us*. We're their friends. It was that fucking simple."

Richie shook his head and held his free hand to his mouth. "It's not that fucking simple," he said. "You know it, Skip. It's not simple."

"No," Skip said, leaning forward, kissing his temple, hushing what seemed to be roiling through him. Well, Skip could sympathize. "It's not simple. But it's huge. Come home with me. We have friends. We can be family. I mean, I met Carpenter's family, Richie—and they weren't perfect. They weren't. They make Carpenter feel like shit even when they're not trying, and I swear, if I ever eat anything called 'tofurkey' again, shoot me before I swallow. But other than their whole vegan thing and pushing out mostly perfect spawn—except for Carpenter, thank God—they were really nice people. But they weren't perfect. And you and me? We're really nice people. We can have a really nice family, even if it's not perfect and what everyone wants it to be, you know?"

Richie gave him a wobbly smile. "You sound really fucking wise, Skipper. You know that?"

"Please?" Skip's voice cracked. "Please? For me, Richie? I mean, you might be able to live this way, but... man, I fucking miss you when you're not at my place. It *hurts*, and I thought I was used to being alone. It's like a few weekends and I'm spoiled—I need you there or my feelings are all messy and bleeding—"

He was going to lose it, start crying like a complete asshole, but Richie cupped his face in his rough hands and kissed him. Oh God, tobacco or no tobacco, Skip had needed the taste of him so badly! Richie deepened the kiss, and Skipper wrapped his arms around Richie's shoulders and gathered him in, taking his tongue and then giving back, needing that ebb and flow, that perilous shift between who was giving and who was getting. Needing it more than water, more than food, more than breath.

Richie moaned and broke away, burying his face in Skip's shoulder.

"Please?" Skip begged again.

"You'd better fucking mean it," Richie threatened, his voice as raw as Skip's.

"Never meant anything more," Skip said, his heart almost breaking with relief.

"C'mon," Richie ordered, grabbing his hand and pulling him toward the back entrance of the garage. "Let's go get my clothes."

They'd taken five, maybe six steps toward the big yellow house when Richie's dad burst out of the front door.

"Richie!" he yelled. "Richie! Dammit, who's out here with you?"

"It's Skipper, Dad," Richie said back. He stopped and clutched Skip's hand so tightly, Skipper wouldn't have dreamed of letting go.

"Skip—what in the hell!" Richie's dad rounded the corner, and Skip could see that the strain of the past few weeks hadn't been kind. His ginger hair was now mostly gray, and there was a lot less of it. Like Richie, he'd lost a little bit of weight, but Ike had lost it in his neck and cheeks. Suddenly Ike Scoggins didn't look like a junkyard bulldog anymore. Suddenly he looked like an old man.

Oh God. Richie must be so torn.

"Hi, Mr. Scoggins," Skip said weakly. Richie was clutching his left hand, so Skip held out his right hand to shake.

Ike Scoggins spit on the ground and growled. "You faggot piece of shit—you get the fuck away from my boy!"

"I'm taking him home." It was funny how those words were maybe the bravest thing Skipper had ever said.

"You're *what*?" Ike strode forward and Skipper braced his knees. He'd done this before already today, and he was fully ready to do it again.

But Richie surprised him. He let go of Skip's hand so he could jump between Skip and Ike, then furiously crossed his arms. "He's taking me home," Richie said clearly.

And all of that bulldog-mean bluster just froze.

"Richie, get back in the house."

"No."

"Richie, I said get back in the—"

"Why?" Richie cried. "So Kay can lie some more about why her little brother didn't show up? So we can listen to your sister talk about the last guy she slept with? I'm *done*, Dad. I'm *done*. Rob and Paul, they pretty much stole your fucking business, you know that?"

Ike seemed to shrink in front of them, and he looked away. "We don't know that—"

"We do too." Richie glowered at his father. "We do know. And all your bullshit about me needing to be taller and stronger, and Kay's bullshit about how I'm too much a smartass to be any good—it's just that. It's bullshit. Everybody's favorite meatsacks ran off with the money, and you know what? I'm the only way you've got to keep your business afloat. And you can keep hiring me to do that right up until the cops shut you down for aiding and abetting and insurance fraud and all sorts of things that can happen if you don't own up to Rob and Paul and what they did. Or you can fire me because I'm gay."

Ike's swing would have leveled his son, but Skip whirled Richie around and took the brunt of it on his shoulder.

Still fucking hurt, but Skip jumped in front of Richie to block the next punch anyway.

It fell, but at half speed, and Ike Scoggins backed off, looking confused in the light from the porch, and Skip barely grunted as it landed.

"Richie, I don't care what this fucker made you—"

"I'm gay," Richie said, louder this time. "And I'm in love. Skipper treats me… like a man should be treated by someone he cares about. He listens when I talk. He makes sure our house is nice—"

"*Our* house—"

"Yeah. Our house. I decorated it. We're getting new tile. I'm going to get him a dog for Christmas, and we're going to make sure it's trapped in the yard. *We're in love*, Dad. Don't you get it? Like you and Mom used to be a long time ago? That's how we are. But we're going to make it, because Skipper's loyal. And he's kind. And he just doesn't ditch out on people. That's not how he's made."

"Get out," Ike said, his voice empty. "Get the fuck away from me. I fed you, I kept you, I fucking *raised* you, and this is what you do? You run off with some cocksucker when I need you the most?"

"If you don't want me to work for you, yeah, Dad. That's how it's going to be."

The tension faded a moment. And then Richie grabbed Skip's hand again. "C'mon, Skip. We're getting my clothes."

"Over my dead—"

Richie pulled out his phone. "I'll call the cops, Dad. You made me sign a lease—it's in the shop, remember? I sign a lease, I have the right to get my clothes. I have the right to get my shit, and if I call the cops, they're going to remember you, and they might start asking more questions about Paul and Rob, and the next thing you know, your precious business is *over* because you were too goddamned mean to let your son get his own fucking clothes."

Richie was snarling, spitting and pissed, by the time he'd finished speaking, and his hand in Skip's felt hot, burning up, with the anger that had been blazing in him all these years.

And Ike Scoggins was a broken man. He turned away, waving his hand.

"Get your shit, Richie. You've got until after dinner, and if you and your faggot boyfriend ain't out of here, I'm telling Kay's *other* brother what you two are doing up there."

"We're not doing *anything*," Richie muttered, "because if we had to have sex in my bedroom with all of you downstairs, my *balls* would deflate."

Ike made a half-strangled noise and started to turn around, but Skip urged Richie on, pushing at his shoulders until they were both walking up the stairs above the garage.

RICHIE WAS right. It didn't take long. He grabbed a couple of garbage bags from the garage, and together they threw all his clothes and blankets in those. He had a few things on his dresser—pictures of himself when he was a kid, pictures of his parents when he was a baby, even some pictures of Kay and Ike and the boys.

Richie grabbed them all, but not carefully, and Skipper wondered where they would hide those things so he could forget that his family had been as broken as Skip's.

They were just shoving the last of the load into their cars when Skip heard a muffled "What in the *fuck!*" from inside the house.

A group of people burst on the lawn in Skip's rearview, just as he and Richie were pulling away. Skip had a momentary worry that they'd tried to follow, but Richie had said Kay's people were all talk. When nobody chased them down, Skip had to guess he was right.

He was relieved.

It was going to be their first night living together and not just playing house.

Skip knew it couldn't be perfect, but he was hoping it would be a start.

THEY STOWED a lot of Richie's shit in the garage but managed to bring most of his clothes inside. After a few frantic moments of shoving it into drawers and finding room in the closet, they were done.

Richie was—ta-da!—moved in.

And both of them were starving.

Skip toasted them some bread and butter and panfried some sausages to put on top.

They dug into the repast without hesitation. Skip was halfway through before he told Richie that he'd been planning to stuff a tiny turkey and do garlic mashed potatoes and sweet potato pie and brussels sprouts and cheese and about six other things, all on Saturday after they'd gotten back from the game.

Richie shook his head and reached for another helping of sliced sausages and cheese. "Nope," he said, throwing a sausage slice into his mouth. "You can do all the fancy shit before Christmas. We'll invite Carpenter, Jefferson, and maybe Jimenez and Cooper, since they don't do much on the holiday, and you can cook for us until we all get fat, how's that?"

Skip grinned at Richie, thinking he looked good in the kitchen, but Skip wanted to try him out other places too. The couch would be good, possibly, but the bed was his ultimate goal. Definitely. Definitely the bed.

"Yeah," he said, feeling some of the wonder of that. "We can... we can have a real Christmas, and people will come over, and...." He swallowed, some of his ebullience fading.

Richie reached across the table and covered Skip's hand with his own. "What's wrong?"

Skip shook his head. "It's... you know. Just... stupid dreams you have when you're a kid. You're going to be a movie star or an astronaut." *You're going to be an athlete and have tons of friends and someone at home who cares if you live or die.* "But this... this, you and me—it's nothing I ever dreamed of, you know? But it's all I ever wanted."

Richie's smile was slow and shy. "Yeah?"

"Yeah."

"Me too." His smile faded and he grazed Skip's cheek with his thumb. "You've got a black eye, do you know that?"

Skipper shrugged and felt the bruise where Mr. Scoggins had nailed him grab his upper arm. "Apparently today was the day everybody wanted to beat the shit out of me," he said and then grimaced, because that was not entirely the truth. "Okay. That's sort of a lie. I hit McAlister first."

Richie gaped. "You hit him first? Jesus, Skip—what'd he say?"

"I don't remember," he lied, brow knitting as he felt very stubbornly that he wasn't ever going to repeat that. "But it wasn't nice."

Richie moved his fingertips from Skip's cheeks to his battered knuckles. "Look at you, Sir Galahad."

Skip flashed him a grin. "You've been playing *The Order*, haven't you?"

"Yeah." Richie's voice dropped and he raised Skip's knuckles to his lips. He pulled back and flashed another one of those shy smiles. "You, uh, came straight over from practice?" he asked delicately.

Skip looked down at himself, soccer slides over his socks, mud pretty much smeared from his ankles to his hips. "Oh God. I *cooked* like this!" He gestured in horror, and Richie laughed.

"Yeah. You came over to face my dad in your soccer slides and your sweats. Man, I'm going to remember that for*ever*. But you don't need to keep the same outfit on that long."

161

Skip stood up in a hurry. "Yeah, uh… I'll be back in twenty."

Richie bit his lip, still smiling. "No hurry. I'll do the dishes while you're drying off." His smile widened. "Turns out I live here!"

Skip nodded, and he had to turn away or he'd kiss Richie while he was all stinky and muddy and… and almost tearful. Richie lived here. His clothes were in the drawers and his chosen flower arrangement was on the table. He'd be there in the morning on Saturday, and on Monday, and all the days in between.

"Out in twenty," he said, proud that his voice didn't shake.

He threw his clothes in the hamper and hit the shower, seeing the plain white tile and the mildew in the corners as he went. He leaned his head against the wall, suddenly frightened all over again. *Oh, Richie. How am I going to make a home for you? It's all I dreamed of as a kid, but all I had as a kid was dreams.*

He thought he'd about conquered that moment of uncertainty when the shower curtain pulled back and Richie stepped in. Skip wiped his face on his upper arm and tried to turn a smile on him, but Richie shook his head and wrapped his arms around Skipper's waist, leaning his cheek against Skipper's back.

"Did you just get scared?" he asked, barely loud enough to carry over the water.

"It just hit me," Skipper said. "I want to give you a home, and I *think* I know how, but, you know. Don't have a really good road map."

Richie laughed a little. "You didn't know how to coach when you started either," he said, tightening his hold. "I'm starting to think being a grown-up isn't going to school or even paying your own rent. It's learning to fake it when you got no other choice."

Skipper laughed too, reassured. "Well, then we're good," he said, turning carefully in Richie's arms. "I've got no choice here, Richie. I tried to imagine us not together anymore, and… it hurt so damned bad. It's what made me come get you. I stand by that."

Richie dodged so that Skip was getting all of the water on the back of his neck and none of it hit Richie in the eyes. "Don't ever imagine life without me," he said soberly. "It makes me hurt inside that you had to do that."

Skipper was tired of hurting. He was ready for joy.

He lowered his head and captured Richie's mouth, smiling when he tasted toothpaste. Richie must have brushed his teeth when he was done with the dishes, which was thoughtful.

"No more cigarettes," Richie whispered against his lips. "I promise."

Skip nodded, but he was done with words. He kissed Richie again, sweetly, and again, hard. He kissed him thoroughly, and then he teased. Richie followed him ravenously, plastered against his front so tightly not even water could get through, and Skip pulled back for a breath. "Did I get all the mud?" he asked, because he had vague memories of soaping up his pits and his privates before he'd lost his shit.

Richie looked down and laughed. "Give me the washcloth, Skipper. You've got mud so far up your legs you practically hit your good bits."

Skip handed it over and turned around automatically. Then the soapy warm washcloth ventured up his thigh, right under his buttocks, and he grunted.

"I didn't think I got mud that high," he said, laughing breathlessly.

"Well, that *is* near your dirty bits," Richie chuckled. He leaned against Skip's arm and kissed his shoulder. His arm shifted, and that warm soapy cloth ventured near forbidden territory again. Skip grunted and pressed up against the tile again.

"Water's gonna get cold soon," he breathed, but they'd gone for what felt like forever without touching like this, and every nerve ending was on high alert.

"Yeah, well, gotta get everything."

Skip looked into Richie's eyes and grinned a little, and Richie skated a fingertip down his crease. "Ooh…." He shuddered, pressing against the shower wall again. Richie very carefully pushed his wet fingertip in, and Skip's cock grew painfully hard against his thigh. "You, uh, thinking you might want to try something tonight?" he asked, smiling at the thought.

"Not tonight," Richie told him, wiggling that finger around some. "Sorry, Skipper. I missed you inside me."

"Yeah, well, I can see why." Skip clenched and squeezed him out, turned the spigot off, and reached outside for towels. He handed one to Richie and the two of them dried off and stepped out of the tub.

They walked naked to the bedroom, and Skip turned to Richie with a wry twist to his lips. "That's nice," he said. The bed had been turned down, and there were clean hand towels, as well as their little bottle of lubricant, on the end table. "It's like we're honeymooning."

Richie nodded. "I just… I don't ever want you to think you can have a better dream."

No. "No," Skip whispered, cupping Richie's neck and pulling him in for a kiss that could *finally* go somewhere. "No better dream than this."

Oh, at first he had the strength to go slow. Richie liked slow, liked the way their skin felt as Skip lay on top of him and glided, chest to chest, kissing and nibbling at his neck and tonguing the curve of his ear. But they were so ripe that the stroke of Skip's hand down Richie's hip made him gasp. He arched his chest up, thrust his nipple into Skip's mouth, and Skip devoured him, pulling and tasting until Richie bucked against his thigh.

"Skip!" Richie keened. "We can't go slow. Not now. I need you."

Skip scrambled up, his cock dripping and bobbing as he moved. Richie started to get up too, but Skip put a hand flat on his chest and shook his head. "Gonna watch you," he said, remembering Sunday night. Yeah, some nights were good for back to front, but he didn't want that now.

Richie nodded, eyes big. They hadn't turned off the lights, and Skip noticed every knotted muscle down his ribs, every lean, stringy inch of him. He'd lost weight these past two weeks and Skip liked him fatter, but God, his pale, pale skin, his ginger hair— so beautiful.

Skip grabbed the lube and Richie clutched his thighs to his chest. Skip winked at him and ran his hands down the backs of Richie's thighs, then parted his cheeks and dove in, pegging with his tongue, swirling, shaking his head playfully until Richie beat gently on his back with his heels.

"Don't be an asshole, Skipper, I really need to be fucked."

Skip pulled back and laughed, his face glazed with his own spit, and then he dumped lube on his cock and stroked it around.

"I ever tell you that I like your dick?" Richie asked, a devil's grin on his face.

"My dick?"

Richie nodded, licking his lips. "I like the length, I like the width, I like the color...."

"The color?" Carefully, Skip positioned himself until he could feel Richie's springy muscle ring, slack and threatening to give.

Richie nodded and tilted his head back. Skipper watched his stomach muscles work as he strove to relax, to accept, to welcome.

"Most especially I like it in my ass," Richie breathed and bore down, taking Skip in one swallow.

Ohh... oh. Oh dear Lord. Skip squeezed his eyes shut and rocked backward and then forward. "I missed this," he breathed. "Is that weird?"

"Not as weird as me missing you right here." Richie said, relaxing into Skip's rhythm. "Oh... damn.... Skipper, you wouldn't wanna go a little faster, would you?"

Skip grabbed Richie's thighs and hoisted him up so his knees were bent over Skip's shoulders—and rocketed his hips forward at speed.

Oh man. It was like he'd been set free. Richie sprawled, abandoned, beneath him, his noises getting louder and higher as Skip pounded hard and fast and without inhibition, his heart thundering like it was going to burst.

Richie's hands clenched in the blankets, and he shot, the white semen landing on his stomach, across his chest, on his chin, a look of profound joy contorting his face as it spattered. Skip fell forward on his elbows, his orgasm washing through him, his hips still not getting the message as he groaned in the hallow of Richie's shoulder and came.

His breathing labored so hard in his chest he saw spots, and as the world became a thing again, he was aware that Richie was murmuring things to him, kissing his temple, stroking his neck and his shoulders, nuzzling his cheek. Skip returned the soft touches, the hushed words.

"Mm...."

"Yeah."

"Good."

"Yeah."

"Skin's good."

"You're still inside me."

"Belong here."

"Stay."

"You too."

"'Kay. We'll stay."

Their breathing returned to normal, and Skip slid to the side, laughing a little, twining his fingers with Richie's after Richie had rolled to *his* side and mirrored his position.

"What do you want to do tomorrow?" he asked, smiling under the light.

"Wake up here."

Skip couldn't stop smiling. "After that?"

"Breakfast and soccer."

Skip smiled so widely he had to squeeze his eyes shut. "After that?"

Richie moved a little closer and licked the end of his nose. "Christmas ornaments," he said. "We'll decorate the place for Christmas, and then in the spring, we can replace that awful tile in the kitchen."

Skip practically vibrated with happiness. "And on Monday?" he asked, not even sure what he was hoping for.

"I get myself a suit and start shopping for a job," Richie said, sounding breathless himself. "Damn. I'm going to have myself a job *not* working for my dad."

And that was it. The happiness seeped into Skip's bones. He stilled and opened his eyes.

Richie was still there, looking at him like between the two of them, they held the magic charm that could make the world bright.

Maybe they did.

THEY WON the game the next day, when they probably shouldn't have. Carpenter was shaping up to be a really good defender—a few more laps, a few more calisthenics on nonpractice days, and he'd be gold. But later, during pizza and beer, the team agreed that Skip and Richie had sort of stolen the show.

"You boys were on *fire!*" Thomas chortled, washing the fire down with a big gulp of beer. "What the hell was that? It's like your big gay secret is out and you guys can't miss a shot!"

"Sh!" Skip held his finger to his lips. "Don't let the other teams know or *all* the forwards will start banging each other!"

Much hilarity ensued, followed by another swig of beer.

And when they wrapped it up, with the general assent of "Same Bat-time, same Bat-channel," Skip had that glow, that reassurance, deep in his stomach. Rec league soccer, yeah. But these guys weren't going away.

Sunday they spent their time doing what Richie suggested. They went out into the frosty morning and hit the tree lots, and came back with a five-foot tree to put in the corner by the television. Then the real work began, and they hit Target and the dollar store for lights—indoor and outdoor—and tinsel and decorations, as well as fake snow to put over the top of the flat screen so they could sprinkle it with glitter.

Richie did his magic thing again with the dollar store and some ingenuity. He came out with a bunch of birthday party Hacky Sacks patterned like soccer balls—about twelve of them. They spent half an hour cutting little holes in the tops and sliding curling ribbon in so they could decorate their tree with soccer balls, since that was what brought them together.

Skip made hot chocolate and they watched *Mad Max 2* in the front room that night, and tried to make a list of what should and should *not* be a Christmas movie. (*Mad Max* was, alas, stricken from the list, but it was decided the first four *Die Hard* movies could stay.)

It was a start, and so was Richie finding Christmas music on Spotify and playing it while he gave Skip what he called "a Christmas blow job"—complete with whipped cream—while Skip sat on the couch and lost his mind.

That was one Christmas tradition he could get behind.

They strung the Christmas lights on Monday, while Richie told Skip about job prospects—and so obviously tried hard *not* to tell Skip about the five hundred million calls he'd ignored from his dad while he was doing that.

Skip asked about it anyway, when they were done stringing the lights. Then, still standing outside as the light faded over the houses across the street, he hugged Richie quietly as all of Richie's fears, his love, his hurt, spilled out in a rambling tirade of epic proportions. Skip let it. Richie needed to talk about it—all of it—or it would forever be lurking behind his eyes when they were trying to build a life. Skip needed to know the extent of the ruins while he laid the foundation.

At last Richie wound down, right when the timer for the lights kicked in. They were still outside under the fruitless mulberry tree, the one Richie had hung the maimed plastic dolls on during Halloween. They'd strung lights around it and hung big plastic decorations that lit up, and as quickly as the tick of a clock, they were surrounded by the wonder of bright lights against a dark sky.

Richie looked up and around and then smiled, the tension and trouble on his face melting. "Look what we did," he said, delighted.

"Yeah," Skip said. The lights down the street must have all been set for six o'clock too, because in the same moment the entire block lit up, and they were out under the moon, surrounded by twinkles and dreams. "Look what we did."

Richie raised his chilled face for a kiss then, and Skip obliged. The hurt was still going to be there—Skip still mourned his mother and the life they might have had if she'd been able to keep it together.

But the ruins there weren't going to destroy him, and the rubble of Richie's old life wasn't going to either.

They just had so much potential to build good things.

By the end of the week, Richie had found a temp job, and while not ideal, it was a source of income he could be proud of, and it would do. They lost their soccer game that Saturday, but they were still riding the flush of Richie's job, and they didn't care. By the end of the pizza and beer, they'd figured that Carpenter, Jimenez, and Thomas (who had just broken up with his girlfriend and moved back in with his parents), as well as Jefferson *and* his mother, were all shoving themselves in Skip and Richie's tiny house for Christmas Eve.

Richie told Skip as they were leaving that they should probably get lawn furniture and a fire pit, or at least a kerosene heater, and that way people could go outside if they wanted.

Well, what the hell. Skip had a deck, right?

They hadn't won enough games as a team to enter the tournament the week before Christmas, but nobody seemed to hold a grudge. What was important was that the team was signing up for second session, ready to start after New Year's. They broke up pizza and beer the night of the last game of the season with a hearty round of toasts to everyone's good health and happy holidays. Skip and Richie made bread to give to everybody who *wasn't* coming to their house for Christmas Eve, and every loaf was well received.

They drove home tired but happy—and making a list between them of what had to be done before they had all that company over in a week.

Richie's dad's truck was parked in front of their house when they got home.

169

And to All a Good Sports Night

SKIP FOUGHT the temptation to yank on the steering wheel and drive around the block. This man had attacked him the last time they'd seen him. He'd tried to hurt Richie. He'd set his relatives on the two of them.

Skip wanted to run away from him and never let him speak to Richie again.

But Richie had finally answered a phone call the week before, and the one thing he'd learned before he'd had to hang up or scream was that his father's life had fallen completely apart. He hadn't wanted to press charges against Rob and Paul, so his insurance claim was invalid. His business was gone, and Richie's stepmom had moved out, so apparently his family had completely disintegrated as well.

He'd been angry on the phone, spitting invective at Richie, at Skip, at gay people and faithless women, pretty much all in the same breath.

But when the matter of his life had been sifted from the dust of his anger, what remained was precious little of value. Skip felt bad for him, and he didn't blame Richie for feeling the same.

Still, he pulled up to the garage warily, parking next to Richie's car and making sure to get out first in case Richie's dad was in a violent mood. Richie trotted after him, slowing to close the garage door, as Skip approached the front porch.

"If you're here to throw another punch," he said evenly, "I will call the cops. This is a nice neighborhood and they don't need any violence out here."

Ike Scoggins's face contorted like he was ready to just *be* that violent, but he relaxed it again after a moment. The fight seemed to drain out of him, and he looked around dispassionately at the lights on the tree and lining the edges of the roof.

"Sure looks like a couple of fairies would be living here," he said, and then his face did this ghastly thing that made Skip think that was an attempt at a joke.

"Yup," he muttered. "All we need are dresses and wands. Can I do anything to *help* you, Mr. Scoggins? I am all about Richie not getting hurt ever again, so it would be great if you could get to the part where we don't have you arrested for being on our porch."

"I'm not here to talk to you," Ike said, growling. "I want to talk to my son."

"I'm right here, Dad," Richie said. "Nice move with the garage door, Skip. That thing sticks."

"Not nice enough to keep you from having to deal with this," Skipper muttered. Then, to Ike: "I'm not leaving you alone with him."

"Fine. Stay there and listen. Fat lot of good I hope it does you." Ike glared at him and then turned his attention to Richie. "Son... my whole life... you heard me the other day. I got nothing. I got no wife, no business. I'm selling the house so I have enough money to live. Are you really going to leave me like this?"

Richie looked at him, torn, and Skip offered his hand. Richie took it.

"You're welcome to join us for Christmas Eve," he said, looking at Skip like he was begging forgiveness. "We're going to have a bunch of people—you could come."

"I want you to come home!" Ike roared. "Don't invite me to a fucking Christmas party that's probably all... whaddayoucallum, gay people anyway! You're my family!"

"I'm Skip's family," Richie said, squeezing Skip's hand and looking at his father with longing. "You're welcome to join us, but I'm not leaving him to come be your little kid again. I mean... I'm sorry. I'm sorry your life fell to shit. There were...." Richie blew out a breath. "There were a lot of things you could have done to not have that happen, but who am I to judge. But I've got a *good* life here. I'm...." He glanced at Skip, his face wearing some of the same wonder he'd shown the night they'd installed the lights. "I'm happy," he said quietly before turning to his father. "I'm not giving Skip up for you, okay? I'm not giving up being gay for you. I'm sorry. You want family for Christmas, you've got to be the kind of man who can love the family he's got."

Ike Scoggins looked at the two of them and shook his head. "You should have been normal," he grunted. And then he turned and left.

Skip and Richie watched him get into his battered red truck and drive away without another word.

THAT NIGHT Skip kept the lights off and managed to make it slow. He kissed every inch, sucked on every pleasure point, hit every spot. When Richie begged, he gave, and when Richie demanded, he took. By the time he was done, they were both drenched in sweat, even in the chill of the room, and Richie was lying limply across his stomach.

"Skip?"

"Yeah?"

"Not that I'm complaining about that or anything, but you've got the job."

Skip smiled. "Excellent. It's gonna be a while before I can apply again anyway."

Richie rolled off of him and flopped over on his back. "You've said that before, but I'm telling you, that thing does not seem to be defective in any way."

Skip grinned into the darkness. "Well, maybe you're just a master mechanic, you know that?"

Richie sat up—just sat right up in bed. "You know what?"

"What?" Skip asked, rolling over to one elbow.

"I *am* a master mechanic. I mean, I *am*."

Skip smiled and rubbed Richie's stomach, just for fun. "I know. You took all the classes, Richie. I mean, I stayed in the tech department, but you've got way more mechanic's classes under your belt."

Richie nodded. "Yeah, but I was applying for all those jobs in my sport coat and slacks and shit, and I wanted the job *you* had."

Skip wrinkled his nose. "The job I have is sort of boring." He'd been thinking about this ever since playing golf with Carpenter's friends. "I mean, I've been thinking about going back to school, maybe getting a business degree or something. Maybe even...." He smiled shyly, because he'd been talking to Thomas about this during beers. "You know, a real degree, and a teaching certificate."

Richie looked at him, eyes wide. "Oh, Skip—I think that would be... I mean, not easy, because... you know...."

"Gay. I hear you. But it's getting easier, right? But that's not for a while. I'm sorry, I interrupted. Tell me what *you* want. And it's not to wear a suit or a polo shirt or any shit like that."

Richie nodded excitedly. "See? You hit it on the head. I think I need to ditch the suit and go get me a real job."

Five days before Christmas Eve, he went out wearing a nice sweater and jeans. He showed up at Skip's work just in time to meet Skip and Carpenter as they left the building for lunch. He was so excited he was hopping on his toes. He'd gotten a job managing an auto parts store, making twice as much as he'd made for his father.

Skip picked him up—just scooped him up and whirled him around in front of Tesko. Richie held out his arms and pretended to fly, and just as Carpenter was snapping a picture that he swore he was sending to his parents, a good-looking guy with silver wings in his dark hair wearing a suit that probably cost Skip's mortgage walked past them.

He paused as Skip let Richie slide down to the touch the ground, though, and Skip caught his gaze and blushed.

"Schipperke!" Mason said, genuine enthusiasm in his voice. "And this must be Richie?"

"Yessir," Skip said, happy. "Come meet him. Richie, this is Mason—"

"Gentleman Caller," Richie said dryly, since they'd taken to calling him that before the chance meeting on the golf course. "Pleased to meet you." He stepped forward to shake hands, though, and Mason smiled at him pleasantly.

"Yeah—it's good to see you here. Last time we talked, Skip was missing you something fierce."

Richie's smile was unguarded, so broad it was almost goofy. "Well, we live together now, so I'm lucky he's not sick of me."

Mason inclined his head and met Skip's eyes gravely. "Good," he said softly. "You... Richie, you keep hold of this one. He's a good one."

Richie nodded. "You think I don't know that?" Richie looked up at Skip with what Skip could only call adoration, and Skip blushed. "He's the *best* one." He smiled at Mason guilelessly. "Which you probably guessed since you kept trying to hit on him."

Mason laughed. "True story. But now I've got no more excuses."

"Nossir, I don't suppose you do. This one's mine. Get your own."

Carpenter let out a slow guffaw behind them, and Skip blushed. "Uhm, Richie, that's not necessary. Mason?"

"Yeah, Schipperke?"

"Oh God—I'm going to start yapping when you do that. I was just thinking—I mean, you said your folks were back east this Christmas and it was you and Dane. You, er, you're both welcome to our place Christmas Eve. We've got a bunch of guys from our soccer club, and their girlfriends, and Jefferson's mother—"

"I did not know she was coming," Carpenter said, sounding impressed. "Well done, Skipper. Jefferson will love you forever."

"Yeah, well, he wanted to get out of the house," Skip said, remembering their brief, intense conversation after the game—and their time at Disneyland, when Jefferson had seemed to need to be free and happy almost as bad as Richie.

"So, party at your place?" Mason said, interrupting wistfully.

It was almost like he needed friends.

Well, Skipper knew the feeling. "Absolutely. Call me after lunch, okay? I'll give you the address. Dates welcome—it's a small place, but we're friendly."

And Mason Hayes, erstwhile pain in Skip's ass, became a friend. "Well, it's good to have friends," he said, shaking on it. "I'll get your details after lunch. Now go—you're going to be late!"

"Yessir!"

They took off at a jog then, and Carpenter kept up. A slicing, soaring wind swooped out of the sky and between the buildings, and Skip, who was in the lead, was just so damned happy that he spread his arms like wings and whooped like a little kid flying down the sidewalk.

As he approached the sandwich place, he looked into the plate glass and saw Richie and Carpenter behind him, arms outstretched too. He laughed as he grabbed the door, and gave them crap for being his flock of loons, but the truth was, he felt like a real Skipper.

Somehow he'd sailed his team to a really happy place.

SO THEY had company, and something to celebrate come Christmas Eve. They gave their guests bread baskets (with more bread) and cookies, and it turned out that the fire pit and the outdoor furniture had been a really good idea. The lot of them ended up outside roasting marshmallows, singing Christmas songs quietly into the night. Carpenter crashed on the couch—he was going to visit his family in the morning—but everybody else went home, and Skip and Richie were left whispering in the quiet of their room deep into the night.

"So Jefferson was interesting," Richie said, eyes alight in the glow from the strings of Christmas lights coming in through the window.

"What was interesting about Jefferson?" Skip asked, yawning.

"He and Mason were *totally* flirting!"

Skip grunted. "Bullshit! Jefferson's not gay!"

Richie laughed, low and gurgling, probably trying not to wake Carpenter. "Oh yeah, and I'm sure he said the same thing about us for, like, *years*."

Skip thought about it and chuckled. "Well, yeah. But we *were* gay. We just didn't know it."

"We knew it," Richie said, nodding. "Every time I think about that conversation in the car and how you thought you just didn't get hard—man, that was a *big* lie. You were just undressing the wrong people with your mind, that's all."

Skip's grin was *not* going away. "Yeah, right. So now I'm a horndog and I won't leave you alone. You complaining?"

Richie shook his head and buried his face in the comforter, apparently too happy about their sex lives over this past month to even pretend it hadn't been awesome. "Not complaining," he said, voice dropping. Then: "So when do we put out Carpenter's present?"

They'd gotten him brand-new shin guards and pads, because he'd been wearing Skip's old gear for the whole season. They'd also gotten him a soccer ball with little hamburgers over it, so he could take comfort in the fact that they knew him for his weaknesses and still loved him.

"Give it another half hour," Skip said. "And let me go—"

"'Cause you've got a gift for me you want to put under the tree," Richie said, nodding.

Skip grunted. "It's nothing that big." It wasn't, really—some books with home improvement ideas, and two tickets to go skiing in February, because home improvement was great but sometimes going someplace fun was good too.

Richie smiled beatifically, like a little kid, and stroked Skip's cheek with that one knuckle. "It'll be great. You're good at gifts. Everybody loved the baskets with the cookies and the bread."

Skip caught his hand and kissed *all* the knuckles. "Well, it's fun to give presents. Fun to have someone to give them to."

Richie sobered. "It's okay, right? The thing I got for you?" he asked for the umpteenth time. He'd actually talked it over with Skip, because he'd been afraid Skip would be depressed or disappointed or something. "I mean, I know you wanted a dog, but I figured I'd get you... you know, dog trappings, and we could go find a dog at the shelter and sort of fall in love with him."

He moved so he could rest his head on Skip's shoulder, and Skip toyed with his recently shorn ringlets. Oh how he hoped Richie would let it grow long again, now that he was starting his job on the twenty-sixth.

"No, that's fine," Skip whispered back. His chest was filled with the most delicious sort of contentment, the sort of suffused sweetness that was *definitely* not the marshmallows. "That's a really good idea."

"You think?" Richie rolled over and propped his chin up with his fist, regarding Skip intently, and their chattering over Christmas suddenly became very serious. Skip had known—even though Richie hadn't said a word—that he'd been hoping his father would relent and show up tonight after all. Ike hadn't shown and Richie hadn't complained, but it was the sort of hurt Skipper couldn't take away.

This worry, though. *This* worry, he could definitely manage.

"Yeah," Skip said decisively. "You know, we can get to know a dog really, really well before we bring him home. Sort of like with us."

"With us?" In the glow from the Christmas lights out front, Skip could see Richie's lips twitch.

"Yeah. *We* knew each other really well before we decided to play house, so we'll do that with a dog."

Richie squinted at him. "I'm not sure if you're kidding or not."

Skip laughed, not sure himself. "It worked out," he said, eyes twinkling.

"Yeah," Richie said with some satisfaction. "It did. Merry Christmas, Skip. Here's to rec league soccer and a brand-new year."

"And to teammates who play for the other team," Skip said, knowing he was earning himself a pillow smack in the head.

Richie kissed him instead, and that was even better.

AMY LANE is a mother of two college students, two grade-schoolers, and two small dogs. She is also a compulsive knitter who writes because she can't silence the voices in her head. She adores fur-babies, knitting socks, and hawt menz, and she dislikes moths, cat boxes, and knuckle-headed macspazzmatrons. She is rarely found cooking, cleaning, or doing domestic chores, but she has been known to knit up an emergency hat/blanket/pair of socks for any occasion whatsoever, or sometimes for no reason at all. Her award-winning writing has three flavors: twisty-purple alternative universe, angsty-orange contemporary, and sunshine-yellow happy. By necessity, she has learned to type like the wind. She's been married for twenty-plus years to her beloved Mate and still believes in Twu Wuv, with a capital Twu and a capital Wuv, and she doesn't see any reason at all for that to change.

Website: www.greenshill.com
Blog: www.writerslane.blogspot.com
E-mail: amylane@greenshill.com
Facebook: www.facebook.com/amy.lane.167
Twitter: @amymaclane

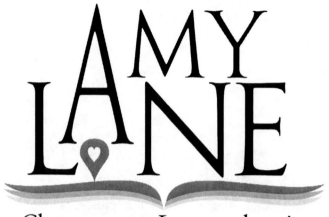

Choose your Lane to love!

Yellow

Amy Lane Lite
Light Contemporary Romance

Available at
www.dreamspinnerpress.com

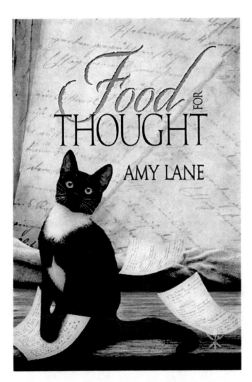

A Tale of the Curious Cookbook

Emmett Gant was planning to tell his father something really important one Sunday morning—but his father passed away first. Now, nearly three years later, Emmett can't seem to clear up who he should be with—the girl with the apple cheeks and the awesome family, or his snarky neighbor, Keegan, who never sees his family but who makes Emmett really happy just by coming over to chat.

Emmett needs clarity.

Fortunately for Emmett, his best friend's mom has a cookbook that promises to give Emmett insight and good food, and Emmett is intrigued. After the cookbook follows him home, Emmett and Keegan decide to make the recipe "For Clarity," and what ensues is both very clear—and a little surprising, especially to Emmett's girlfriend. Emmett is going to have to think hard about his past and the really important thing he forgot to tell his father if he wants to get the recipe for love just right.

www.dreamspinnerpress.com

Every dreary day, Zach Driscoll takes the elevator from the penthouse apartment of his father's building to his coldly charmed life where being a union lawyer instead of a corporate lawyer is an act of rebellion. Every day, that is, until the day the elevator breaks and Sean Mallory practically runs into his arms.

Substitute teacher Sean Mallory is everything Zach is not—poor, happy, and goofily charming. With a disarming smile and a penchant for drama, Sean laughs his way into Zach's heart one elevator ride at a time. Zach would love to get to know Sean better, but first he needs the courage to leave his ivory tower and face a relationship that doesn't end at the "Ding!"

www.dreamspinnerpress.com

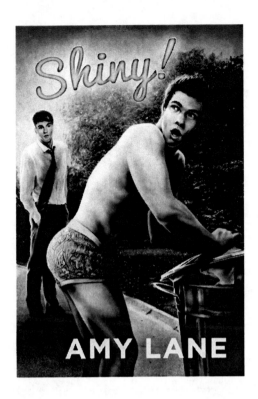

Will Lafferty and Kenny Scalia are both having sort of a day. Will gets fired for letting fifth graders read Harry Potter, and Kenny finds his boyfriend and his sex toys in bed with a complete stranger. When Will knocks over Kenny's trash can—and strews Kenny's personal business all over the street—it feels like the perfect craptastic climax to the sewage of suckage that has rained down on them both.

But ever-friendly, ever-kind Will asks snarky Kenny out for a beer—God knows they both need one—and two amazing things occur: Kenny discovers talking to Will might be the best form of intercourse ever, and Will discovers he's gay.

Their unlikely friendship seems like the perfect platonic match until Will reveals how very much more he's been feeling for Kenny almost since the beginning. But Kenny's worried. Will's newfound sexuality is bright and glittery and shiny, but what happens when that wears off? Is Will's infatuation with Kenny strong enough to stay real?

www.dreamspinnerpress.com

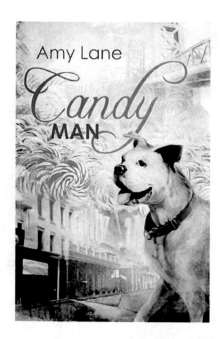

A Candy Man Book

Adam Macias has been thrown a few curve balls in his life, but losing his VA grant because his car broke down and he missed a class was the one that struck him out. One relative away from homelessness, he's taking the bus to Sacramento, where his cousin has offered a house-sitting job and a new start. He has one goal, and that's to get his life back on track. Friends, pets, lovers? Need not apply.

Finn Stewart takes one look at Adam as he's applying to Candy Heaven and decides he's much too fascinating to leave alone. Finn is bright and shiny—and has never been hurt. Adam is wary of his attention from the very beginning—Finn is dangerous to every sort of peace Adam is forging, and Adam may just be too damaged to let him in at all.

But Finn is tenacious, and Adam's new boss, Darrin, doesn't take bullshit for an answer. Adam is going to have to ask himself which is harder—letting Finn in or living without him? With the holidays approaching it seems like an easy question, but Adam knows from experience that life is seldom simple, and the world seldom cooperates with hope, faith, or the plans of cats and men.

www.dreamspinnerpress.com

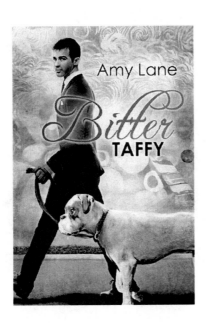

A Candy Man Book

Rico Gonzalves-Macias didn't expect to fall in love during his internship in New York—and he didn't expect the boss's son to out them both and get him fired either. When he returns to Sacramento stunned and heartbroken, he finds his cousin, Adam, and Adam's boyfriend, Finn, haven't just been house-sitting—they've made his once sterile apartment into a home.

When Adam gets him a job interview with the adorable, magnetic, practically perfect Derek Huston, Rico feels especially out of his depth. Derek makes it no secret that he wants Rico, but Rico is just starting to figure out that he's a beginner at the really important stuff and doesn't want to jump into anything with both feet.

Derek is a both-feet kind of guy. But he's also made mistakes of his own and doesn't want to pressure Rico into anything. Together they work to find a compromise between instant attraction and long-lasting love, and while they're working, Rico gets a primer in why family isn't always a bad idea. He needs to believe Derek can be his family before Derek's formidable patience runs out—because even a practically perfect boyfriend is capable of being hurt.

www.dreamspinnerpress.com

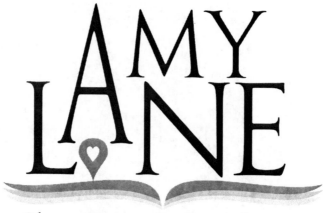

Choose your Lane to love!

Orange

Amy's
Dark Contemporary Romance

Available at
www.dreamspinnerpress.com

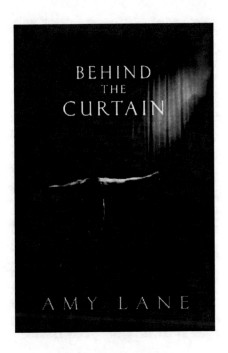

Dawson Barnes recognizes his world is very small and very charmed. Running his community college theater like a petty god, he and his best friend, Benji know they'll succeed as stage techs after graduation. His father adores him, Benji would die for him, and Dawson never doubted the safety net of his family, even when life hit him below the belt.

But nothing prepared him for falling on Jared Emory's head.

Aloof dance superstar Jared is a sweet, vulnerable man and Dawson's life suits him like a fitted ballet slipper. They forge a long-distance romance from their love of the theater and the magic of Denny's. At first it's perfect: Dawson gets periodic visits and nookie from a gorgeous man who "gets" him—and Jared gets respite from the ultra-competitive world of dancing that almost consumed him.

That is until Jared shows up sick and desperate and Dawson finally sees the distance between them concealed painful things Jared kept inside. If he doesn't grow up—and fast—his "superstar" might not survive his own weaknesses. That would be a shame, because the real, fragile Jared that Dawson sees behind the curtain is the person he can see spending his life with.

www.dreamspinnerpress.com

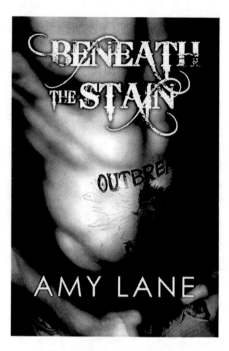

In a town as small as Tyson, CA, everybody knew the four brothers with the four different fathers—and their penchant for making good music when they weren't getting into trouble. For Mackey Sanders, playing in Outbreak Monkey with his brothers and their friends—especially Grant Adams—made Tyson bearable. But Grant has plans for getting Mackey and the Sanders boys out of Tyson, even if that means staying behind.

Between the heartbreak of leaving Grant and the terrifying, glamorous life of rock stardom, Mackey is adrift and sinking fast. When he's hit rock bottom, Trav Ford shows up, courtesy of their record company and a producer who wants to see what Mackey can do if he doesn't flame out first. But cleaning up his act means coming clean about Grant, and that's not easy to do or say. Mackey might make it with Trav's help—but Trav's not sure he's going to survive falling in love with Mackey.

Mackey James Sanders comes with a whole lot of messy, painful baggage, and law-and-order Trav doesn't do messy or painful. And just when Trav thinks they may have mastered every demon in Mackey's past, the biggest, baddest demon of all comes knocking.

www.dreamspinnerpress.com

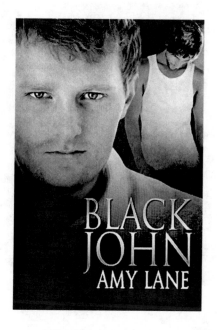

Johnnies: Book Four

John Carey is just out of rehab and dying inside when he gets word that Tory, the guy who loved him and broke him, has removed himself from the world in the most bitter way possible—and left John to clean up his mess.

Forced back to his hometown in Florida, John's craving a hit with every memory when he meets Tory's neighbor. Spacey and judgmental, Galen Henderson has been rotting in his crappy apartment since a motorcycle accident robbed him of his mobility, his looks, and his boyfriend all in one mistake. Galen's been hiding at the bottom of an oxy bottle, but when John shows up, he feels obligated to help wade through the wreckage of Tory's life.

The last thing John needs is another relationship with an addict, and the last thing Galen wants is a conscience. Both of them are shocked when they find that their battered souls can learn from and heal one another. It doesn't hurt that they're both getting a crash course on how growing up and getting past your worst mistakes sure beats the alternative—and that true love is something to fight to keep if your lover is fighting to love you back.

www.dreamspinnerpress.com

CPSIA information can be obtained
at www.ICGtesting.com
Printed in the USA
FFOW03n2354200316
22436FF